Serendipity

Casie L. Williams

Get Colin's Exclusive Journal Entry After Meeting Jo

Go to CasieLWilliams.com to download!

ACKNOWLEDGEMENTS

I cannot express my thanks to everyone who has helped me along this journey. Michael, Robin, Devon, Katelyn, and so many more who have believed in me even when I did not believe in myself. Thank you all so much.

Contents

Prologue

"Alexa, play soft ballads from the 80s," I stated as I sat on the floor in the middle of my master closet. I was surrounded by the daunting task of spring cleaning. I hated spring cleaning. It never seemed to end. I always have way more crap to get rid of than I expect. Talk about anxiety; I have to psyche myself up for like a week before I even get started. You would think by now I wouldn't have an issue, but I do.

Alexa began playing Guns 'n Roses as I continued to sit and stare blankly at the junk piled up. Pulling my knees up and resting my head on them, I just listened as Axl Rose belted out the words to "Sweet Child O' Mine." Taking a deep breath, I hear the words, "Sweet child,

Sweet child of mine," finishing the song.

"Well, this crap won't clear itself out. Might as well as get to it."

I stood up and started with the top shelf. I pulled down an old shoe box full to the brim with pictures and trinkets. The lid was just sitting on top, not even properly on because it was so full. Just as I was lifting the top, Jon Bon Jovi's voice began low and slow, and I saw a picture of me laughing and instantly I was transported back to The Screaming Eagle bar.

Chapter 1

"Boy Dale, you sure can tell when it's be-

tween paydays," I sighed, wiping down the top of the nearly empty bar for the umpteenth time.

"Yup, it's slower than a herd of turtles. Enjoy it, 'cuz next weekend you'll be runnin' all over hell's half acre." Dale sat at the end of the bar smoking his cigarette while watching some sports commentary.

Just then, a small party of soldiers came bustling in. They were talking to a new guy.

"Yeah, this is the best waterin' hole around. Can't beat the prices," someone stated.

I was watching to see how many as I started popping water glasses on the bartop and filling them and that's when I really saw the new guy.

Damn.... Hold it girl, he's a soldier, chillax.

"Hey guys, here's some water to get ya started. Know what ya want?" I asked, placing the water glasses along with a pitcher in the center of the table.

I looked up as a few local college girls came barging in while Pat Benatar's voice bellowed over the speakers. They started smiling when they saw the high and tight haircuts and I knew what they were thinking—soldiers!

The new guy had a great smile and was being friendly, talking to the coeds who were basically throwing themselves at the guys.

Really, don't you know you sell yourself short by givin' up the goods without getting to know the person properly?! Oh well, your life.

Watching the scene unfold, I began to roll my eyes. *Typical soldier, willing to go after anything in a skirt.*

I watched the two parties to see if they needed refills, my impression of the new guy quickly eroding as I watched the interaction. Except that he kept trying to steal glances at me.

Finally, the new guy came up to the bar. I figured it was to order another round. I gave my bartender smile,

"What can I get ya, darlin'?" I call almost everyone darlin'.

New guy smiled and almost seemed to blush a bit. His smile widened and he gave his name, Colin. I noticed how great his smile was, but checked myself, remembering the unabashed flirting going on between him and the coed who was eyeing me with daggers.

"What is your name, miss?"

"Jo."

Smiling all the bigger, a hint of dimple surfaced. "Another round please? Also, more water," he said, and headed back to his party, but not before doing a bit of a sideways glance back showing his crooked smile and his steel-grey captivating eyes.

Cool it girl! He's just another soldier with a great smile and amazing eyes, with a great

butt… No! Stop it now! Get his order and be done, girl!

I got the water and beer and brought them to the table. Colin made a point to stop paying attention to his coed friend and asked, "Where are you from?"

Coed bitterly huffed.

"Born and raised right here," I answered quickly and left.

The nerve of that guy. Shamelessly flirting with one girl and then flirting with me right in front of her. Hope that girl doesn't invite him back to her place.

I went back to the tables a few times over the course of the evening, picking up empty beer mugs and seeing if anyone needed refills. Meanwhile the few regulars at the bar slowly left, leaving Dale at his seat still smoking and watching another sports commentary and the soldiers with the coeds chatting away.

Every time I went by, Colin would smile or grin and ask me a random question or make some comment. And every time I answered politely and referred back to his 'friend', asking or saying something about her.

"Thanks, how's your date goin'?" "So how do you two know each other?" Anything to let him know I wasn't interested in being one of his first conquests at the base.

Finally, Colin came up to the bar and leaned with crossed arms on the bartop. He started saying something, but by this time I was tired of watching him flirt with the coed and me simultaneously. Plus, I was so ready for my shift to be done.

"Look, I've tried to be nice, but you don't seem to be getting the hint," I said finally, frustration leaking into my tone.

Confusion swept his face. I grabbed the soda gun and pressed the water button, spraying him. That's when Dale took notice and came over.

"Everythin' ok, Jo?" His undeniably-protective stance made Colin back away, shaking out his hands.

"It's ok, honest mistake."

"Hey, why don't you knock off early? I can close up. It's last call anyways. Serious, hun, head out." He always called me hun. He was way more than a boss; he was like an older brother, always making sure I was good and taken care of. He was my only family.

I took him up on the offer and headed home to forget the whole night.

****

Weeks passed and I had all but forgotten that night, though Dale sometimes gave me a wink when I was using the soda gun. I usually just rolled my eyes or elbowed him as I walked past. He was a big brother pickin' on his little sister. A basic pain in the arse at my expense.

It was a typical Friday night—regulars socializing, jukebox playing, the sound of pool balls clinking and conversations rising in volume the later it got and the more drinks were consumed. By ten, it appeared we would have another weekend without soldiers. I couldn't have been more wrong.

Without warning, a group of fifteen to twenty already rowdy—not drunk—guys came bursting through the doors. Their haircuts gave them away: soldiers out for a night of fun and letting loose.

"JO!" several yelled in unison.

"Hey fellas, been awhile. Kinda missed ya," I answered, smiling as I put the glasses and pitchers of water I had grabbed when they came in and watching as they pushed together five tables.

"Where ya been?" I asked no one in particular.

A guy answered, "Training for what seems like ever." His smile caught me off guard; my mind did a mental stumble. I recognized him, but I hadn't remembered his smile being so charming.

Regaining my faculties, I said, "Alrighty guys, most of you know the house rules, but I do see a few new faces." I stared right at my mystery guy. "Hand over the keys and you've already got your water. What are we startin' the night off with? Shots or beer?"

As the guys went searching for their car keys, they animatedly discussed what they would order first. I walked around with the key bucket collecting keys and smiling the whole time. These guys tended to crack me up with their banter. Honestly, I knew how it would play out. Some would say shots, some would say beer and I would suggest my usual.

"What do ya think guys? Beer or shots first?" one guy asked with a goofy side grin. I called it; some wanted shots, some couldn't decide, and others wanted beer. So naturally I offered my suggestion.

"How about I start y'all with a round of what's on tap? Unless you want buckets."

The guys exchanged looks and turned to me all smiles. "Works for us, Jo. *Draft it is*!"

"Not a problem, but as always, I gotta see IDs fellas," I added, smiling and winking as the guys half-heartedly groaned and reached for their IDs. I checked my mystery guy's ID last, Colin Dawson. Unlike the rest, he made sure to hand me his ID while looking me in the eye. When I handed it back, our hands briefly touched, and something sparked between us. I tried to give him a goofy girly smile in response to the spark.

What had begun as a slow night quickly did a 180 with me doing laps around the bar. Dale was handling the patrons and regulars at the bar, leaving me to take care of the soldiers. In the first hour or so, I must have served two or three rounds of draft, refilled the waters twice, and brought a round of shots. Those boys had me running.

By last call, only the soldiers were left. Most were ready to call it, so Dale was making the cab calls while the guys settled their respective tabs. I thought they had all left when I popped my quarter in and selected Bon Jovi's "Bed of Roses". I looked around and saw Colin walking over to the bar with some beer mugs. Smiling, I grabbed some as well and met him at the bar. "You don't have to do that. Go, head back to the barracks. I got this."

"I wanted to stay. This gave me a reason. See, I've been thinking about that night a few weeks back, and have been wondering why you sprayed me." Though he was smiling, there seemed to be a hint of concern, even utter dumbfoundment at not getting me in the sack that night. Who knows.

"To be honest, after working all night and watching you drink and hit on that other girl,

I really didn't want to deal with ya. But you didn't seem to get my subtle hints, so I figured I would make myself clear as crystal," I said as I cleared more glasses.

His silence stopped me mid-step. He had this look of complete confusion contorting his features. Finally, I couldn't take it. "*What*? What is so confusing?"

It came out harsher than I meant, but it was already past two in the morning and I was exhausted. He seemed taken aback by my question and tone.

He looked at me carefully and simply stated, "I wasn't hitting on anyone *but* you that night. Though I can see what you mean. I tend to get that reaction. Sorry for the wrong impression." At that, he turned and walked to the door.

I mentally kicked myself. *Wow, I really put the ass into assumption.* Here was this genuinely nice guy and I was a total witch. I turned and called out, "Colin, wait..." I walked over to him. "I'm sorry. I'm not used to guys just being friendly. I made an ass out of myself. Can we start over?"

Smiling, I held out my right hand. "Hey, I'm Joleene, but everyone calls me Jo. Welcome to The Screaming Eagle, the best hole-in-the-wall bar around."

For a moment I thought he was going to leave me hanging, not that I blamed him.

Then, smiling back, he gently took hold of my hand. "Hi Joleene, I'm Colin."

His smile was so genuine, reaching all the way to his eyes, causing those cute little crinkles at the outside corners. The way his hand felt with the rough calluses combined with how he said my name sent a chill down my spine. It sounds corny, but how he simply said my name and held my hand seemed to stop time.

"Your cab is waitin' buddy," Dale called from behind the bar. And with that, the moment was gone.

"Thanks," Colin replied without ever looking away.

He brought my hand to his lips and lightly kissed it, just as Bon Jovi sang the final line, 'And lay you down on a bed of roses'.

"Good night, Joleene. It was nice meeting you. Maybe I'll see ya 'round." And with that, he headed out to his waiting cab.

Honestly, that was all it took, I was in awe and completely smitten.

"*Jo*! Ya gonna stand there all night?" Dale called, pulling me from my thoughts.

Chapter 2

In the weeks that followed, Colin came in nearly every weekend, making sure to catch my eye when he came in. He would figure out where I was that night and 'park' himself where I would wait on him. I still laugh thinking about those nights. On the nights where it was crazy busy, I still made sure to stop and say hi, and when I did he would take hold of my hand and gently kiss it saying, "Hi, Joleene."

I know I would smile like a giddy schoolgirl, but I didn't care. Colin was amazing and everything I was told to look for in a guy. Kind to others, a gentleman, sweet, gentle, respectful even to those who weren't so to him. He always seemed able to make me smile and blush, and the kind of guy I never really truly believed existed.

When Colin would show up, it was the highlight of my night. Though one time I asked him, "Why do you only order a soda?" His response took me back a bit.

"Honestly, I am not that big of a drinker. The night we met was a rarity. In fact, I think I have only ever drank like that one or maybe two other times." He chuckled and bowed his head, looking at me somewhat from the side in that 'aw shucks' look.

I remember on one of my nights off, I was at my friend Layla's place talking.

"Seriously, who does that? Who goes to a bar every weekend, orders soda only and wants to talk to *me*? I mean come on, what guy do you know who wants to be friends with a girl and get to know her before even asking her out on a date? Don't get me wrong, Layla, I am so lovin' it, I'm just not used to it is all."

Grinning, Layla just sat there for a moment. Finally, she gave me her two cents,

"Well, the way I look at it, you can either accept the attention or you can tell him to bugger off. But if it were me, I would let things play out. Enjoy the attention and see where it leads. But that's me, you do what you want," she finished, looking at me as she raised her wine glass and took a sip.

Chapter 3

"Hey, Colin," I grinned as I placed a beverage napkin with his usual Coke on top in front of him on the well-worn bartop. He returned the grin.

My heart began racing as it did every time I saw that crooked smile.

Calm down, Jo. He hasn't even asked you out. Chillax.

"Hi Joleene. How's it been?"

"Not too busy. Fairly steady. You? How was your week?"

"Long. Weapons checks and extra PT in the afternoon. Then briefings and death by Powerpoint, then more weapon checks. Boring really." A corner of his mouth hitched up into his amazing crooked smile as he half chuckled before taking a sip of his soda and giving me a wink with his steel-grey eyes.

Goodness, why do his eyes do that to me? I'm sure I look like one of those coeds who throw themselves at anyone in a uniform. That's why he hasn't asked me out yet. Duh!

Smiling, and blushing, I mentally shook myself from my revelry, pretending to wipe down the bar and hoping my thoughts weren't plastered across my face.

"Hey Joleene, I would really like to take you out to dinner sometime. Could I?"

Pretty sure my mental double take showed through, because Colin seemed to straighten a bit.

"It's ok if not. I probably seem kinda creepy hanging out here every weekend. Forget I said anything." He quickly took a sip so try and hide his dismay.

I mentally kicked myself for showing my shock. *You're an idiot. Why not just smile and tell him yes, you moron. That's what you've*

wanted. Now you've got him thinking you're not interested. Stupid! Say something! Quick!
"Sorry, Colin, I would love to go to dinner with you. I didn't mean to seem like I wasn't interested. I just... I don't know, sometimes I'm an idiot. And then I turn into a babbling idiot." I laughed nervously at my own gibberish.

"I would love to go to dinner," I said more calmly, making sure to look him square in his amazing steel-grey eyes while trying not to hold my breath.

"I'm sure that is not true. You could never be an idiot, let alone a babbling one," he said, winking as he took another sip.

****

Ring! Ring! Ring!
Fumbling around her nightstand, Layla was trying to see through her eye mask to locate the thing screaming at her. Finally, her hand connected with the screaming and vibrating noise box. Pushing her mask up just enough to pry open an eyelid, she slid the 'answer'

button. Before the phone even reached her ear, Jo's voice came through:

"LAYLA! He did it! He finally did it! He actually did it! I can't believe he did it!"

Layla yawned audibly before mumbling, "Gr-great, what? Who? Huh? Who did what?"

"Colin. He asked. Me. OUT!" Jo shouted through the phone.

"*Girl*! That's awesome and I want the deets, but can it wait 'til at least I've had some coffee? Seriously, what the hell time is it?" Layla asked, yawning through a half smile and rubbing her eyes to get them to focus.

"Oh sorry, I was just way too excited to sleep in this morning. Tell ya what, I'll grab the lattes and be over in fifteen. That should give you a chance to at least wash your face."

Not even giving her a chance to decline, Jo said bye and hung up.

Chapter 4

I was so excited. I felt like I was walking on air. I was going on an actual date with Colin. Like a real date, not just him coming to the bar where we exchange a few words in between me taking care of other customers. But a real date!

Eek!

Tuesday night couldn't come soon enough. I was a ball of energy and nerves at the same time. No, Tuesday isn't your typical date night, but I worked most Friday and Saturday nights, so...

We pulled into the parking lot of O'Charley's, a great steakhouse nestled right at the juncture of the Red and Cumberland rivers. There was a gorgeous backdrop to go with the amazing food.

Colin parked, got out and came around to open my door. I smiled as he took my hand to help me out of his white Jeep Wrangler. We walked up to the entrance, his hand just above the small of my back, guiding me. Then he opened the big door. "Ladies first."

The young man waiting to seat us gave us a half smile. "Patio or inside?" was all he said. Not exactly the warmest greeting, but honestly, I didn't care.

"Do you mind if we sit on the patio? It's nice out," I asked.

A smile graced Colin's lips. "That sounds perfect, patio please."

The host led us to a table by the rail where we had a nice subtle breeze and the soft sounds of the river below. I couldn't have imagined a better scene for our first date.

Colin pulled out my chair.

"I've never had anyone do that. Thank you," I said beaming while taking my seat and nervously tucking my hair behind my right ear. It was an unconscious habit.

"That's a shame, but I'm glad I was the first one to treat you like a lady," he said, his crooked grin growing wider.

His smile always made my tummy flutter, but now those butterflies were having themselves a dance party.

"This is so nice," was all I could muster. *So dumb, Jo. This is so nice?! Really?*

"It really is. I've actually been wanting to check this place out since I got here, so I knew this is where I wanted to take you. Though it never occurred to me until now— are you a vegetarian?"

I could hear the nervousness in his voice at the idea he may have inadvertently brought a vegetarian to a steakhouse.

"No, I'm not." I giggled at his concern. "No, I love this place. But I don't think I've been out here. My girls and I usually sit at the bar and I try not to critique the bartenders."

"Really? Well I guess that's an occupational hazard." He chuckled and I could see his shoulders visibly relax.

Just then the waiter showed up. "Good evening, my name is Todd. I'll be helping you tonight. What can I start you with? Perhaps a refreshing twisted lemonade or maybe a frozen strawberry daiquiri?"

"Actually, the daiquiri sounds great, but can you make it virgin?" I asked as I held the menu.

"Sure. And you sir?" He turned slightly towards Colin.

"Ya know, I always like a refreshing drink. Think I'll have the same." He smiled first at Todd and then turned that gorgeous heart-stopping grin towards me. I swear my stomach was trying out for the Olympics.

"Got it. I'll give you a few moments to look over the menu while I put in your drink order." With that, Todd turned and left.

Looking up from my menu I saw Colin staring at me. Just looking at me. He was wearing a clean-cut black t-shirt tucked into a pair of *very nice* fitting jeans and a black Stetson to finish off the look. Normally I would've been like, *Really jeans and a t-shirt for a first date? Seriously buddy?! Def no second date for you.*

But Colin just looked... exquisite. I found my-self wondering what it would feel like to be in his arms. Then looking at his crooked grin, his lips seemed so kissable... *Chill girl. It's only the first date, you don't want him to think you're easy.* By then Todd had dropped off waters so I quickly grabbed my glass and took a sip and wondered what Colin was thinking.

Reaching for our glasses at the same time, we both giggled at the simple action.

"Joleene, you look amazing. I mean you al-ways do, but... wow! I'm gonna shut up now before I really swallow my foot." Colin seemed to answer my question concerning his thoughts before taking a gulp of his water. Maybe he was just as nervous as I was?

"Thank you. Yeah, I normally don't wear a dress to work," I said, beaming from his com-pliment.

Before long simple quick glances gave way to easy casual conversation, from favorite colors to how we ended up in this town.

When Todd stopped by to get our order, we realized we hadn't even looked at the menu.

"No worries, I'll get your daiquiris and be right back to get your order."

"Guess we better take a look.   " Colin grinned.

"Guess so." But looking at the menu was the last thing I wanted to do. I quickly decided on the six-ounce sirloin dinner and put the menu down.

Colin seemed also unable to concentrate on the choices. He kept looking at me, his eyes scanning across my hair and face.

Todd returned a few moments later and set our daiquiris down in front of us. Colin still hadn't decided. I gave my order and then Todd turned to Colin.

"And you sir?"

"Ya know, that sounds delicious," he said, looking at me. "Think I'll have the same."

Todd wrote down the order and headed back in.

"Couldn't decide, could you?" I asked, winking at him and grinning.

"How could you tell?"

"Because there was a bit of a lag after I gave my order before Todd asked for yours," I explained, grabbing my daiquiri and chuckling.

"That obvious," he said, grinning. "You have a delightful laugh, Joleene."

I could feel myself blush. The heat rising over my cheeks. I wasn't used to getting compliments. Colin definitely was a gentleman.

The conversation flowed as we learned more about each other. Every time he gave me a compliment, I instinctively tucked my hair behind my ear, even when it wasn't out of place. His eyes followed the motion, and there was a warm endearment in them as he did so.

Neither of us really registered the food had arrived as we grew more comfortable with each other.

I was so taken by Colin's crooked smile. Sometimes, as I found myself looking at him, my breath would catch. His eyes had glints of gold as he smiled. And I knew I was blushing every time he gave me a compliment, but I didn't care. I just tucked my hair behind my right ear again and smiled.

We paused when Todd checked on us and took away the now- empty plates.

"How was everything?" he asked as he stacked the plates.

"Great!" we both answered and then laughed.

"Good, I'll be back when you're ready to pay." Todd set down the bill holder and backed away as our conversation resumed.

Colin pulled out his wallet and paid the bill. Then stood up. I was bummed the date was ending so soon, but knew he had to get up early for PT the next morning.

I gathered my purse just as Colin came up behind to hold the chair.

"Thank you," I said, standing and again tucking my hair behind my ear. "I'm sure you have an early morning." I secretly wanted the night to go on and also wanted to feel his hand in mine.

Just then, as if reading my thoughts, Colin softly grabbed my hand and led me to the river walkway. "I do, but I still have some time," he said, not even bothering to check his phone for the time.

Oh wow. His hand is so strong and yet gentle. It feels so warm and comfortable, I thought as Colin laced his fingers with mine.

"So, how are you liking Fort Campbell?" I asked.

"It's been pretty good. The guys haven't hazed me too bad..."

And like before, the conversation drifted with ease.

Before long the sun had completely set and the stars had begun to twinkle.

"Oh goodness, it's getting late. I hadn't realized the time." I began searching in my purse for my phone. "Wow, it's almost ten, we should head back to your Jeep."

Colin's eyes became downcast and his smile slipped a bit. "Yeah we have a ruck march tomorrow."

"That doesn't sound fun."

"It's not," he chuckled.

Walking back to his Jeep, we held hands and enjoyed the comfortable silence again.

Colin opened the door and waited for me to get situated. It was apparent neither of us wanted the evening to end.

On the way back to my place, the conversation picked back up. A couple times one of us would make a comment about the song on the radio and he would either turn it up or down.

Before either of us wanted, we were at my apartment complex. Colin parked the Jeep and came around to the passenger door.

He truly is a one-of-a-kind gentleman. A girl could get used to this, I thought.

Holding hands, Colin walked me to my door. I had never felt so special.

I wondered if he would kiss me. I wanted him to, but again didn't want to come off as easy. Finally, Colin leaned in and planted a slow and sweet kiss on my cheek. I couldn't help closing my eyes as his lips graced my skin. When our eyes met, I could see how much he liked me. I only hoped he could see the same in mine.

Chapter 5

As Colin drove back to the barracks, he found himself unconsciously turning off the radio and letting his thoughts take over, replaying the entire evening. The conversation, the way she looked in her simple lavender dress, how the sunlight reflected in her eyes. The tint of pink in her cheeks as she smiled and blushed, her shoulder-length, golden-brown hair softly brushing her shoulders. My goodness, she truly was gorgeous. Colin loved how Joleene would tuck her hair behind her right ear, even when it wasn't out of place, whenever he complimented her. The slight coloring to her cheeks told him she might not be used to compliments, but he was only speaking the truth. He was completely enamored with her.

Honk!

Someone was blaring their horn, snapping Colin from his revelry. He continued driving, his thoughts quickly drifting to her laugh. Oh man, her laughter was so infectious. She was beautiful inside as well.

Before he knew it, he was at the main gate. He turned his lights down to his runners and reached for his ID. As he rolled up, handing over his ID, the other soldier checked it and walked around the Jeep, then wished Colin a good night.

Back on his way, Colin began thinking of Joleene's hand in his as they strode down the river path, the way her fingers naturally intertwined with his, without a single thought. Holding her hand was beyond words. *Mmmmmm... it felt so right. How her hand fits in mine.* He came to his parking lot by his company and found a parking spot, some distance from his barracks. But honestly he didn't care. It gave him more time to think about walking Joleene to her door. After helping her out of the Jeep, he captured her hand. He didn't want her to go. Part of him wanted to pull her to him and kiss her, but he thought better of it. Instead he held her hand as they walked to her door. He tried to keep her close without stepping on her toes. He could feel her body warmth and smell her soft lavender scent.

Oh, I should have said something about how great she smelled or something. Colin started as he stopped short and sidestepped the oncoming night sergeant who was making his rounds.

"Oh, hey Sergeant. Sorry. My mind was somewhere else."

"A bit late, specialist."

"Yes, sir. Lost track of time, but set for tomorrow already, Sergeant."

"Good deal. You best be going, zero 400 comes fast."

"Yes, sir."

Getting to his door, Colin thought, *Sergeant's right. I best be getting to bed, but Joleene's skin was so soft ...* and his thoughts began to drift as he quietly unlocked his barrack's room believing Kimber was asleep.

"Dude, how was it?" Colin's roommate, Isaac Kimber, caught him off guard as he walked in. "Oh you're awake?"

"Yeah." Kimber was finishing packing for the ruck march in the morning while "The Last Witch Hunter" played for sound. "Just getting everything around. Tell me how'd it go?"

"Man, it was great. She is amazing."

"Really?!" Kimber lifted his eyebrows and gave the typical 'Ah yeah, brotha I know what you're sayin.'

"Just stop. Nothing happened. We talked and went for a walk on the river bank. We held hands. Hell, I didn't even give her a kiss." Colin felt he had to make sure Kimber didn't think ill of Joleene.

"So, let me get this straight, you didn't even kiss her and yet you think she's amazing?" cocking one eyebrow in disbelief.

"Yes. It is possible to go on a date with a woman and not have sex." Colin shook his head and began making sure his ruck sack was in order. "Dude, whatever, believe me or not. I'm gonna double check all my gear is ready then hittin the sack."

"Alright, chill. I'm just bustin your chops." Kimber raised his hands in surrender all the while smiling from ear to ear. "Yeah, I'm all set just packing up. Night."
"Night."

Sergeant was right, 0400 came faster than Colin would have liked. He stumbled through getting ready, trying to wake up. The crisp air smacked him as he left his room. His eyes popped open fully and he found himself ready for the task all soldiers hate: ruck marches. But this was to qualify him for his EIB, expert infantry badge. He wanted it. He was ready.
By mile 18, Colin found himself fighting fatigue—mental and physical—focusing on his breathing and keeping his rhythm. His thoughts drifted back to the night before.
He held onto Joleene's hand. Oh, how perfect her hand felt in his, their fingers intertwined together. So naturally as if they had been together for years.
Once they got to her door, he remembered lingering for just a moment. He wanted to kiss her but didn't want to scare her off. So

he merely grazed her cheek. She smelled so good. The lavender scent was still fresh to him. He could almost smell it. That's when his thoughts really began to wander into dreaming.

I could have walked slower to her door, or better, held her hand lingering a bit more at her door, or...

He saw himself turning to face her before she reached for her keys, reaching up with his left hand and sliding it to the back of her neck and tangling his fingers in her hair, staring into her eyes...

"Damn Dawson! Where the hell'd you come from?" Kimber shouted as I passed him at mile 22. I hadn't even realized I was passing him until he said something and tossed me the chem-light, signifying I was the leader for the march.

Tucking the glow-stick in my helmet, my thoughts went back to Joleene. Her hazel eyes really weren't hazel, but more green with flecks of gold. They didn't twinkle but were so full of joy.

Maybe sparkled would have...would be a good way to describe them. No, that doesn't fit them either.

He could stare at them and get lost for days. Slowly, he found himself leaning down and just as he was about to capture her lips with his own...

"Ahhhhh damn! What the... Ahhhh, son of—" A pain was shooting down his leg, ripping him from his thoughts. His leg was cramping with a mile left in the march. Stumbling to the side of the road, Colin dropped to the ground to try to stretch out the cramp so he could finish the march and qualify.

"Hot damn!" he groaned, rubbing down his calf.

"You good?" Kimber came up seeing Colin off to the side.

"Yeah, cramp." Colin groaned while rubbing his leg.

"Thought you said nothing happened last night," Kimber jeered

Colin looked up at Kimber as he was getting ready to pass.

"Shut the hell up, Kimber!" Colin threw the chem-light at him, mumbling under his breath how much of an ass Kimber could be. Concentrating on simply walking or rather hobbling, the last mile kept Colin from finishing his thoughts.

Chapter 6

"So...?" Layla was sitting on the edge of her

seat trying to look patient as she waited for
Jo to finish her sip of coffee.

Smiling and watching her best friend about to
fall out of her chair waiting for the juicy de-
tails was priceless. "So, what?" I asked.

"Are you kidding me?" Layla almost shouted;
she had to adjust herself before she really did
fall out of the chair.

"What? It was nice. He was sweet." I was pur-
posefully giving little away. It was too funny
watching Layla.

"That's it? It was nice. He was sweet. That's
all you're gonna tell me? You dragged me out
of bed to tell me that?!" Layla was playing up

the indignation, damn near spitting out her coffee. I coughed at the way she was acting.

"Ok, settle, girl. It was amazing! He took me to O'Charley's. We sat out on the patio and talked and talked. I don't even remember how dinner was. Once we left the restaurant, we walked the boardwalk holding hands. Oh my gosh, the way his hands felt..." My voice drifted just thinking about how natural it had felt to hold his hand. Our fingers entwined. The casual silence that was so comfortable. The conversation that we'd had was as if we'd known each other for years instead of really only getting to know each other that night.

"Ok, give me more, come *on*. I can see it. There's more. *Spill it*, girl!"

"We talked, we walked in silence. We held hands. He walked me to my door..."

"He kissed you, didn't he? I knew it. He kissed you. That's why you are so doe-eyed. He kissed you."

"Yes, he kissed me, but not the way you are thinking. He gave me a sweet kiss on the cheek."

"What? On the cheek? Guess no second date."

"No, it was sweet and perfect. I loved it. I'm tellin' ya, he's a true gentleman. He held the door for me, held out my chair. Girl, I can't describe it. I can't wait for the next date."

We spent the next hour gabbing about this and that, but I kept thinking about Colin's hand holding mine and how sweet the kiss had been.

Chapter 7

The weeks rolled past and summer came.

Colin and I spent as much time together as possible. Weeknight dates and weekend visits by calling into The Screaming Eagle. He held my hand and guided me. We walked dinner dates by the river or at a hibachi grill, movies and walks in the park. But never once did he try to kiss me. In fact, the only other kiss he gave me was on my hand on one of our walks. He brought up my hand that was laced with his and kissed it so softly while standing and staring deeply in my eyes. I thought for sure he was going to kiss me. But instead he continued walking.

Uh...I thought he was going to kiss me. Maybe I seem too desperate or gave the impression I didn't want to go to that level. Oh hell, I don't know!

But I never let these inner thoughts show. I was a little bummed, but I was loving the time with him. How he would guide me in a restaurant or movie theater, how he would reach for my hand as we walked or the smile he gave whenever he'd give me a compliment and make me blush. Oh yes. I loved that smile; it gave my tummy butterflies reason to dance all the more every time.

Mini golf. Who'd say mini golf when asked about a romantic date? No one really, until that day.

Colin took me out on a rare Saturday afternoon date to play mini golf. Not long after we started, the laughter began. I was horrible at putting and Colin, well, Colin, wasn't trying to do anything but watch me and have fun. Which made my putting even worse.

"Really?! How come I can't get the ball in the hole? It's like it has two feet." I grunted as my ball yet again went past the hole for like the fourth time. We were only on the third hole. Colin was trying so hard not to laugh, ducking his head down under his hat. He always wore his Stetson and looked damn good in it too. "Don't laugh. It's not funny. I think my ball is defective."

"I'm not laughing," he said, biting his lip. He was clearly trying really hard not to. "We can switch balls if you'd like."

"Well, after this hole," I said stubbornly.

So Colin walked up to his ball and tapped it. Wouldn't you know it, that little tap sent the ball the four plus feet it needed to sink into the hole!

"That's it. We're switching balls *now*," I said and walked over to the hole, grabbed his ball and stomped over to my ball and switched them. Then I tapped it and it didn't go in; it skidded around the edge and pushed out, rolling four feet before bumping into the edging. "What! Seriously? Okay. It has to be my club," I half laughed at Collin as he just busted out laughing. "Sorry, but I've never seen such *luck* at, at mini golf," he said.

"Glad I'm amusing you," I said with some fake pouting.

Then, Colin strode the ten feet to me, captured my face in his hands and next thing I knew, he kissed me.

This wasn't a simple peck. This was passion. Anyone looking on would undoubtedly swear we were in love. Time stopped. I didn't care where we were or who was around. I dropped my club and, going up on my toes, I reached up and wrapped my arms around his neck. His kiss only deepened.

The sounds of giggles pulled us back to reality. We looked over and saw a couple of schoolgirls watching from the next hole. Both were smiling cutely.

"We should probably continue playing before the next group comes up." Colin softly kissed me again then bent down to grab my club and handed it to me.

I was still too light-headed from the kiss to register what he was saying until he was handing me the club.

We finished playing, though the rest of the day was a bit of a blur.

****

"You a'right, Jo?" Dale was staring at me with an eyebrow raised.

"What? Huh? Oh, sorry. I'm fine." I sounded almost dreamy and continued wiping the same glass I had been cleaning for the last 20 minutes.

"Ya sure?" he pressed.

"Yeah. Why?" I frowned.

"Because you've been kind of dazy-like all night, plus I'm pretty sure that glass is beer clean by now."

I looked down, finally realizing I hadn't been cleaning multiple glasses, like I thought, but only one.

"Yeah. Sorry. My mind wandered," I said, trying to play it off as I put up the very clean glass and grabbed the next.

"Okay. Out with it. What's up?"

"What do you mean?"

"Tell me what's going on." Dale was a bit uppity sounding.

"What do you mean, 'What's going on'?" I immediately began blushing and trying to clean the glasses faster so I could get away from Dale's probing questions and inquisitive stare.

"What happened today? You weren't like this last night and I haven't seen *Loverboy* yet tonight. So spill it. What happened?"

"Nothing. He probably won't come tonight. We went out this afternoon."

"Okay. So what happened?" Dale was beginning to get protective. I could hear it in his voice. He probably thought *Loverboy*, as he called Colin, hurt me or tried something.

"Nothing, honest," I insisted, turning away to clean the bar top at the other end. Anything to avoid talking to him. But Dale wouldn't drop it.

"Jo, out with it. What did he do?" His concern was apparent.

"He kissed me. All right?" I practically shouted from the other end of the bar. The few customers stopped what they were doing to see what was going on, then went back to their own lives when they realized it was nothing.

"He kissed ya?! Ya mean he hadn't yet?" Dale was chuckling and laughing. "So you're all gooey googly-eyed and space-cadety because he kissed ya?" he asked, laughing all the harder.

"See? That's why I didn't want to tell you. I knew you'd make fun."

"Then ya shouldn't've been actin all weird. I wouldn't've known somethin' was up."

I could tell this was only the beginning of what would no doubt be torment for at least the next week.

****

"We were playing minigolf. Well actually he was playing and I was pouting because I couldn't get it in the hole and he kissed me—"

"Wait, what? Slow down girl." Layla was laughing at my babbling.

"Sorry, he took me to play minigolf yesterday and I was having a hard time putting, so I was pouting. Next thing I knew, he was kissing me."

"Like silly kiss you to get you to stop pitchin' a fit?"

"No like world-stopping kiss."

"Oh."

"Yeah"

"So it was good?"

"Omg! That kiss…good doesn't even come close to describing it. Ya know how in the movies the guy just walks over and kisses the girl passionately?"

"Uh huh…" I could tell she was hanging on every word.

"Like that. He literally dropped his club and strode over to me and tilted my face towards his and kissed me. I swear the world stopped. No joke."

"Wow!"

Chapter 8

As the months rolled by, I could tell feelings were growing, though neither of us had verbalized anything. There hadn't been many weeks where we had not gone out; in fact the only times we didn't was when he was in the field training. We had fun getting to know one another. We went to the movies, dinner, get togethers with friends, and even some silly and fun dates at the minigolf park and go-kart track. We spent hours talking and laughing. It was amazing to be with him.

What would most people think of as the best place to hear the words, *I love you*? Restaurant, movies, after an intimate time together. Not many would say the batting cages, except for me. Time flew by; next thing anyone knew, summer was in full swing with the fourth in a week.

Colin and I rarely met up for dates on the weekends with my schedule at the bar. So when he took me to the batting cages on Thursday, late afternoon, it was nearly empty. I was not one to go out for sports in general, but Colin really wanted to go, saying he "missed hitting balls" like he did back home.

He went first to show me how easy it was. I stood behind the fence safely away from fly-ing balls. He missed the very first ball.

"I thought you said you did this all the time."

"Remember it's been a while. So let me warm up before you go busting my chops." He reset himself.

I shook my head thinking he was just being typical over exaggerating his skill to impress a girl.

CRACK! The sound of metal connecting with the ball shut my thought down. And my mouth dropped open.

Lucky shot. He's just trying to prove ...

CRACK! My thoughts were broken by another ball being hit.

Five more booming cracks of impact echoed through the air.

One after another, he hit the ball. I just stood there looking completely dumbfounded.

"I stand corrected."

Colin looked back at me with his side grin and tipped his head down and winked. "Your turn. I've warmed it up for you."

"Yeah. Thanks. I'm good watching."

"Nope. You got to try this. Just hit a couple balls and we'll call it and grab some ice cream."

Ooh, he knows my weakness.

"Okay, fine. But only a couple of balls. Right?" I asked as I slowly made my way around the entrance into the cage.

"Promise. Hit a few and then ice cream." He leaned his bat against the back fence and grabbed the other one. "This should work for you." He handed it to me.

I set myself up while he walked to where I had been watching from.

The machine made a noise and the ball was ejected at what seemed like a thousand miles per hour. I swung and royally missed, practically spinning myself around. I caught Colin, trying not to laugh.

"Nice try. Try again. The first one can be tricky."

Another sound, another ball, another swing. Another miss.

"Okay. Time for ice cream," I said as I set my bat down next to his.

"Not yet."

"But you said a couple of balls. That's two. I tried, I missed. Time for ice cream."

"I said hit a couple of balls. Then we'll go get ice cream."

"We'll be here all night."

"No, you'll be fine. Just square up your feet. Lift the bat with your elbows. Parallel to the ground. When you hear the sound, count to three and swing."

I just looked at him. He's got to be nuts.

Colin, shaking his head and chuckling, came from behind the fence and behind me. Placing his hands gently on my hips he moved them to fit to his, then he wrapped his arms around me and placed his hands over mine on the bat.

"Just breathe slowly. Watch for the pitch. Keep your eye on the ball," he whispered softly in my ear. Closing my eyes, I breathed in his aftershave. Oh, did he smell amazing. Then I heard the ball exit the pitching machine. Opening my eyes and trying again to hit the ball, I missed, nearly toppling us. I was laughing so hard... I almost missed it.

"I love you, Joleene!"

Stumbling from his words, I could hardly believe what I had just heard. *No way, he didn't really just tell me he loves me, did he?* I guess I was looking at him strange for too long, as he began to pull away from me.

"No," I pulled him closer. "Sorry, I didn't expect to hear you tell me that you... that." I choked on the words a bit, not wanting to repeat them in case I misheard.

"Tell you what? That I love you? I do."

"Oh Colin, I love you! I wanted to tell you so many times, but I was afraid I would scare you. Please don't think I don't love you, I do. I was just surprised is all."

Colin looked into my eyes and smiled. Time seemed to slow. He gently slid his left hand to the back of my neck lowering his soft lips to mine. Tenderly our lips touched in the most dulcet kiss imaginable.

Chapter 9

"*So* he said it? He actually said it? He told you he loves you?!" Layla was on the edge of the couch, almost spilling the glass of wine in her hand.

"Yes he did, now watch your glass, girl. Yes, he told me he loves me. Girl, I can't even tell you how shocked I was. I thought I heard him wrong or I was dreaming. Then time just stopped. When my brain started working again I told him I loved him too. And the kiss he gave me... oh my." I was smiling like a silly schoolgirl with a crush. I closed my eyes, the touch of his lips still fresh in my mind.

"It was so soft and sweet. Slow and romantic. Like in the movies. No, not like the movies, better! I could feel his love in the kiss."

Setting her glass on the table and sitting back, Layla just stared at me. A smile crept across her lips.

"So when are we planning the big day, hmm?"

"What? No. We've only known each other a few months. I mean, yeah, sure someday I want to get married, but I am not thinking about that right now and I doubt he is either. No, we aren't getting married." I took a sip of my own wine. I hadn't even entertained the idea of marriage ever, but now that Layla said something...

****

The next morning I couldn't stop thinking about what Layla said. I even dreamt about marrying Colin. *A simple wedding, maybe at a park with our closest friends and his family. I could always talk to Dale to see if we could have the reception at the bar. Hmm... Oh what am I thinking? He only just told me he loved me. Snap out of it, girl! Just enjoy this time. Besides, he will probably get stationed somewhere else soon enough and are you gonna follow him? I mean really? No, not really.*

Chapter 10

Colin had been in the field for close to three weeks and I was working my sixth straight day. I had found picking up extra hours helped pass the time while he was training. Bonus: it allowed me the chance to take some time off when he wasn't training.

I wasn't expecting him back until Saturday afternoon at the earliest. I was cleaning up, following my normal routine, when the jukebox began to play *Bed of Roses.* I knew the bar was all but empty, so I turned towards the jukebox and found Colin leaning against it in his tucked-in black t-shirt and nice fitting jeans. And of course, his Stetson. He tilted his head and gave me his famous crooked smile.

I shook my head and walked over to him. *What a surprise!*

"When did you get back?" I grinned as I got to him and wrapped my arms around his neck. He didn't return the embrace and that's when I realized his smile had vanished. I stepped back. My breath caught in my chest, panic washed over me. He'd been gone for nearly three weeks and unexpectedly showed up.

Oh no, he's going to break up with me. He decided he doesn't want to seriously be in a relationship. This is gonna suck. I love him so much...

My internal rant almost made me miss...

Wait... what's h...

I gasped and unconsciously tucked my hair behind my ear.

Huh? he's... he's down... He's down on one knee. Oh! My! What?

There Colin was on one knee staring up at me. "Joleene Nicole Henderson, will you do me the honor of making me the happiest man and spend the rest of your life with me?"

Honestly, I couldn't breathe. Then I was having a hard time seeing as the tears blurred my vision. Blinking, I finally saw him holding open a tiny black velvet box. Light glinted off the small diamond. I had no words. How could I possibly speak? I couldn't breathe. And I'm pretty sure my brain had fully stopped. I just nodded my head, afraid words would fail me, and held out my left hand.

Chapter 11

Beep, beep, beep, beep, beep...

I hit my phone multiple times to turn off the alarm. I was only partially able to see. Finally I located the spot to stop the annoying sound. I flopped back over, trying to figure out why my alarm was going off. Like I said, I wasn't fully awake, so my brain wasn't firing on all cylinders yet.

"Why did I set my alarm today?" I was rubbing the sleep from my eyes and then a lightning bolt hit me and I sat upright, fully awake. "I'm getting married today!" I was screaming as I bounded from my bed. I grabbed my phone, double checking the time. I was meeting Layla to get our hair done at ten.

Oh good, it's only eight. I didn't oversleep. I was grinning and looking at my lock screen picture. It was Colin and I at the batting cages. I spun around, so happy.

There was a knock at the door that stopped me just before getting too dizzy. I floated to the door in my nightshirt. I so didn't care. Nothing could spoil this day.

"Delivery for Joleene Henderson," the delivery guy stated. As I opened the door, he was holding a gorgeous bouquet of flowers, roses mixed with carnations and baby's breath, which smelled amazing.

"I'm Joleene," I said, reaching forward as the guy handed me the bouquet. "Thank you."

He was already leaving when I called out, "Have a fantastic day."

Closing the door as I smelled the flowers, I smiled. "Who are these from?"

I found the card, but before I could read it, there was another knock at the door. I turned back and opened it and there was the delivery guy holding another bouquet of flowers. Daisies and carnations this time.

"Here you go. Sorry. I can only carry one at a time. Have a great day." He turned and left. Holding both the vases, I used my foot to close the door. "Two bouquets in the same day? Who from?" I wondered aloud, walking to the kitchen bar top. I sat them down. I checked out the card of the daisy bouquet.

> We are all so happy for you and Colin. Here's to an amazing life full of adventure, batting cages and minigolf. Love Layla, Dale, and the rest of the Screaming Eagle family.

Looking at the daisies, again, I just smiled as tears obscured my vision.
My parents may be gone, but I still have my family.
I smelled them one last time before turning my attention to the rose bouquet.

> I do.

That was it. Those two little words opened the floodgates, tears flowed freely as my smile stretched ear to ear. I was going to spend the rest of my life with my true soulmate.

I spent the morning with Layla getting our hair done. Nothing too fancy, just something special. Soft beach waves, loosely tied back and held by a purple rose. The crisp fall breeze graced my arms and legs, leaving small goosebumps as Layla and I walked the steps to the courthouse. No fancy wedding in a packed church, just a simple JP wedding in front of Layla and Colin's roommate Isaac with dinner at The Screaming Eagle.

At least, that's what I thought. I stopped, surprised and curious, when I saw Dale at the top of the stairs, talking to Colin and Isaac. Evidently Colin had asked Dale for permission to ask for my hand and thought Dale should be there when we promised our lives together—him being my only family.

I walked straight into Dale's arms and whispered, "Thank you."

Dale hugged me back. "You're my family too." Dale wasn't much of a talker, but I always understood what he was saying.

Isaac cleared his throat. "Guys. We probably should go in before y'all miss your appointment. Pretty sure that judge doesn't take kindly to people missing their appointments."

"Right," I said, releasing Dale from my bear hug grip.

"Thank you guys for being here. I know it means the world to us." I smiled as I looked at each one.

"Now don't start cryin'. You'll ruin your makeup before even saying 'I do.'" Layla was handing me a tissue to dab at the tear, which threatened to spill over. I had never been happier.

There was nothing lavish or exotic about the ceremony. In fact, it was done in less than twenty minutes, but I didn't care. I was officially Joleene Dawson, and those that meant the world to me were there.

"Pictures," Layla trilled, handing me the small bouquet of purple roses she had gotten me.

"No, it's okay. We don't need pictures." I knew Colin wasn't a big fan of being in pictures.

"Yes. Pictures. We need this and I know you'll want to show our kids." Colin grabbed my hand, leading me outside to the steps. "I know the perfect spot for our very first picture as husband and wife."

Layla, Dale, and Isaac followed, I'm sure snickering under their breath as Colin pulled me with so much enthusiasm. One would have thought he was a kid going to the amusement park. I'm not sure who was more excited. I just followed behind, smiling and laughing at his playful nature.

Outside the courthouse was a modest fountain. Colin led us all to that spot.

"Sit right here, my love, and Layla, will you take the picture?" He sat next to me, grasped my hands and gazed into my eyes. The world stood still. Then he reached over and gave me a soft kiss on my cheek, reminiscent of our first date.

"What a perfect picture!" Layla broke into my little world. I blushed as I remembered we were not alone.

"Okay. Picture of the ladies." Colin beamed at me. Several shots later of me and Layla, and of the guys and even a few with Dale and me, I felt one was missing.

I ran over to another couple who were walking by. "Would you mind taking a couple pictures of all of us please?" I asked, pointing to everyone by the fountain.

"Sure," they agreed and followed me over. They took several silly pictures and one special one.

"Thank you," we said as the other couple gave me back my phone and went about their day.

"Well, that was fun, but I'm starvin'. I'm so hungry, I could eat the north end of a southbound goat." Dale was always so eloquent.

"Yeah, me too, dude. What's for food?" Isaac asked no one in particular.

"We ordered some pizza to be delivered to the bar. Let's go. They should be there soon." Holding Colin's hand, we headed towards his Jeep.

"Isaac, do you mind hitchin' a ride with Layla or Dale? Kinda would like to be alone with my bride." Colin grinned at me.

"Sure. Figured I'd ride with someone. Layla, would you mind?"

"Sure. So we'll meet you two there," she said, winking at Colin and I, "but don't take all night please."

I just rolled my eyes and followed everyone to the parking lot. I gave Layla, Dale, and Isaac a hug before hopping into Colin's Jeep. The Screaming Eagle wasn't too far from the courthouse, so we decided to stop at our favorite park to just walk. As we walked, our fingers entwined, I couldn't help smiling.

"Why are you so happy, Mrs. Dawson?" he quipped with a twinkle in his eye, bringing my hand up to lightly kiss it.

"I love these walks. I love being here with you. I love being called 'Mrs. Dawson'. I love you."

He squeezed my hand and pulled me to him and held me in his arms. I could have stayed there forever.

We continued walking, talking about this and that. And before long, Colin simply stated, "I guess we best be going. Isaac will probably eat Dale out of all of the pretzels." It was clear in his voice it was the last thing he wanted.

I knew how he felt because I felt the same, saying, "Yeah, we should get going, but we can always come back after food." I was still smiling.

We turned back to the Jeep and made our way to The Screaming Eagle. "I just realized I'm quite hungry myself. Hope those pizzas are ready." Colin grinned as he pulled into the parking lot.

He opened my door and grabbed hold of me for one final embrace without onlookers.

"I love you, Joleene Dawson."

"I love you, Colin."

And with that, we walked into a surprise. Layla and Dale had decorated the inside of the bar, set up a buffet, and had eighties music playing on the jukebox. There was even a banner.

Congratulations, Mr. and Mrs. Dawson

There were some purple roses and carnations and faces on the tables and green balloons floating around.

"What is all this?" The tears came without warning at the amazing gesture our friends had prepared.

"We couldn't let you guys not have a reception. So we put one together. I know it's not much, but y'all didn't give us much planning time." Layla and Dale winked.

The bar was still open for regular business, so the few patrons clapped and raised their glasses. Some shouted congrats. Colin walked over to Dale to shake his hand and Dale gave him the 'man hug', clapping him on the back.

Layla came over and hugged me tightly through muffled thank you's which resulted in laughing with tears streaming down our faces.

Behind her, though, I don't think Colin and Dale realized I was paying attention or in hearing distance because Colin said, "Thank you. I know this means the world to her,"

"'tis the least I can do. Oh, and here's something for you to open later." I watched Dale trying to be covert as he handed Colin an envelope, which Colin slipped in his back pocket with a smile and a nod before turning and approaching me and Layla.

"Mind if I hug the maid of honor?" Colin cleared his throat and handed us each a handkerchief.

"Yes, of course. I should go say thank you to Dale anyways." I let her go and gave Colin a quick kiss before heading over to Dale. I decided not to ask about the envelope. Surely, Colin would clue me in later.

The closer I got to him, the more tears that threatened to spill over and obscure my vision. "How can I thank you?" was all I could say. He stood up and wrapped me in a brotherly hug and the floodgates busted open.

"Now, stop that blubberin'. I can't have my sister lookin' all teary eyed and makeup ruined on her wedding day." That only made the tears fall harder. It was the first time he called me his sister. I always knew I was like family to him, but today he voiced it. I couldn't have been happier.

"Okay. Enough with hugs and mushy stuff. Let's eat." Isaac broke through my tears with his boisterous levity.

"Yes, let's eat and celebrate." Colin walked over to Isaac, clapping him on the back.

In turn we grabbed plates and food and sat at one of the larger tables clearly set up for us. We ate, laughed, and talked. Dale gave a little brotherly speech hinting that if Colin broke my heart, no one would find the body. Layla tried to give a speech, but for once was speechless.

Colin stood up. "Thank you all from the bottom of my heart. You all mean so much to us. And I know I can speak for both of us, just this once"—he winked—"we are truly grateful and love you all."

Everyone held up glasses. "Here, here!"

"Cheers," and the clinking of glasses responded. The night continued with small talk, laughter, and celebration.

Colin stole me away from some patrons who were talking my ear off and pulled me to an empty spot by the jukebox and chose "Bed Of Roses".

He pulled me close and began swaying as Jon Bon Jovi's sultry voice could be heard over the bar noise.

I'm not sure if someone put the song on re-peat or if time just slowed in his arms. I laid my head on his chest. I so didn't care. I was happy.

Chapter 12

*L*ife was bliss to say the least. Colin moved into my simple one-bedroom apartment and we began navigating the new terrain of living together as well as husband and wife.

Then the dreaded day we tried to ignore came: November 10th. Deployment orders. We knew eventually they would come, but still, it was a jolt back to reality when they finally did.

The knowing of when they'd head out didn't make it easier to accept. In fact, things got a bit frantic as holiday season was coming up. So certain places on posts would have limited hours until after the new year, then it would be a mad house trying to fit everyone in for the various logistical things all soldiers had to deal with prior to deployment: POA—power of attorney— forms, wills, bills, vehicles, and who knows what else.

"This is why I love you." Colin grinned as I listed everything we needed to get done before the February 10th deployment window.

"This is the only, *only* reason you love me, cuz I need to organize things in order for me to not stress over what needs to be done. Really?" I was mockingly scolding.

"Okay. Part of the reason I love you." He winked at me.

"What can I say? I like to feel in control as much as I can." I shrugged my shoulders.

Over the weeks leading up to Christmas, we tried to deal with as many of the items as possible so we wouldn't be rushed like everyone else.

Thanksgiving was spent with Dale and Layla at the bar. We went to Colin's company Christmas party, but left as soon as we could to go to our favorite park. Our walks were the best. No matter the frigid temps, those moments were warm and perfect.

And before I realized it, December 21st was only a couple of days away and it dawned on me Colin's birthday was that day. Layla and I were planning on Christmas shopping later that afternoon. So I decided to go birthday shopping then too.

But what do I get him?

I had been trying to think of what to get him for Christmas for days as it was. But nothing came to mind. I didn't want to get him only things he needed for deployment. I wanted to get him something from the heart. I continued picking up around the apartment before heading to get Layla.

Damn, I still have no clue. Maybe Layla can help, I thought as I closed and locked the door.

"Girl. We have been all over this mall. What are you looking for?" Layla plopped herself on the chair in one of the seating areas at Opry Mills Mall. She was clearly exasperated by me dragging her through the mall. We hadn't really visited many stores, maybe three or four. We really had been walking the halls of the mall. She would point to one and say, *"What about checking out this store? Or what about here? Or maybe here?"* Most of the time, I barely glanced and shook my head. How could I not know what to get my husband? Not only for Christmas but his birthday too.

"I don't know. Something that shows I put some thought into it. I don't want his first birthday with me or our first Christmas together to seem to have no real significance." I sighed as I slumped into the chair next to her and dropped my head into my hands, mumbling the last few words. "I want this to be special."

"Well, I got nothing for ya. If I had an idea, maybe, but without some input I'm tapped, girl."

I just sat there with my head in my hands, hunched over my knees. *What am I going to do? I've got like two days 'til his birthday and then three more to be ready for Christmas.*

"Come on. We'll walk through again." Layla had stood up and was kicking my foot while picking up her found treasures.

"No, I know you're tired. Let's just go. Maybe I can get some hints from him tomorrow after he gets home."

"Where is he tonight?"

"Twenty-four-hour duty. So he'll be home sometime mid-morning. I can ask him then."

We started on our way back through the craziness of other mall patrons, weaving this way and that trying to avoid getting bumped into by those not paying attention. I twisted to avoid someone who was simply plowing through with little care of others and something caught my eye: black dog tags from Things Remembered.

I grabbed Layla's arm. "We're going in here." I made a beeline for the display. "This is perfect. I'll get this. And by post there's a little kiosk that can scan a picture onto a silver one. This is perfect!" I was so excited. I found one of Collin's presents. We found a clerk who ordered the dog tags.

"Hey, I know which picture you should use. The one I took at the fountain. That's a great one."

"Yeah. Perfect. I'll order it tomorrow while Colin is sleeping. Now to find his birthday gift."

We continued walking through the throng of shoppers. I was reenergized. I had ordered his Christmas present, plus a few extras for fun, but now I needed something for his birthday. Nothing else caught my eye before we left the mall. We stopped to grab some dinner before heading back. What had begun as a near panic trip had turned around. I had a plan for the next day. I hoped I would figure out something tomorrow. I dropped Layla off and called Colin to let him know I was home.

"Hey, love. How's the night been?"

"Fairly quiet. Most of the guys are getting ready for leave or have already left. It's nice, but it makes me miss you more."

I smiled as if he could see me. "I love you and miss you too."

"Hey babe, can you add some notebooks to my packing list?"

"Sure. Why?"

"I use them for journals, and I finished my last one just before the wedding."

"You kept a journal?"

"Yep. I know. Kind of corny or girly, but sometimes I like to go back and remember events. So could you add that to my packing list? I need a new one before I leave."

"Sure. I'm writing it down right now." Secretly my mind was turning.

Journal. Perfect. I know of a place that has a black, soft leather journal. Maybe I could get it personalized or something,

"Babe. Did you hear me?"

"What? Oh, sorry. Something caught my attention out at the window. What'd you say?"

"Just I love you. I gotta go make my rounds."

"I love you too, night. See you in the morning."

"Sweet dreams, my love."

Click.

I had my plan. After Colin got home and went to bed, I would head out to get the second dog tag and the journal.

****

December 21st finally came. I had planned for us to go to O'Charley's for dinner. Of course, it being December, we couldn't sit out on the patio, but we still loved the place. I had his journal wrapped and safely hidden in my purse. I was so excited.

I had missed wishing him a happy birthday before he left that morning. So I was surprised when he came home expecting us to stay in.

"Why are we going out? It's not a special date I forgot, is it?" He seemed not quite panicky, but definitely on the nervous side.

"Well, of course it's a special day, silly. It's your birthday!" I was grinning at him as I walked up to him and gave him a big hug.

"Oh, that's okay, hun. We don't have to do anything special. I usually don't celebrate my birthday because it's so close to Christmas." He kissed me on my forehead.

"That's absurd. This is your special day and deserves some celebration! Go change. Unless you'd prefer to go in your fatigues." I raised an eyebrow to show he could not change my mind.

"Okay! Okay. I'll change. Give me 10 minutes."

"Deal," I said, bouncing on my tiptoes, giving him a peck and grinning.

A while later, Colin sat back in his side of the booth with a smile that stretched ear to ear. He was happy.

"I honestly can't remember the last time I did anything for my birthday. Thank you."

"Well, that's a shame, but I'm glad I'm the one to show you how special you are and worth celebrating." I gave him a wink.

His head dropped as his signature crooked grin poked through. He shook his head. "You remembered."

"Of course! 'The first person to show me how a lady should be treated.' How could I forget?!"

Right then, I reached into my purse and pulled out a metallic blue package and handed it to him. The look of surprise really drove home to me how little he expected of his birthday.

"Joleene, you didn't have to get me anything. Honest." He seemed almost reluctant to accept the present.

"Colin. I wanted this birthday to be special because it's our first together, but I wish I could make it even more special given what you told me."

I reached for his hand and squeezed. His boyish grin turned soft and loving.

"It's perfect," he said after opening the package. He turned the soft black leather journal over in his hands before opening the front cover.

"I'm glad you like it. It's not much. But when you said something about needing journals, I remembered seeing this. I had to get it for you."

"I love it. It's what I always wanted, but never found."

Chapter 13

Christmas morning was quiet. We stayed in bed until 10. It was so nice to just cuddle and relax. No alarms beeping, trying to arouse us from slumber. Just the sound of the heater kicking on. I mean it was Christmas in Kentucky.

I made cinnamon rolls for breakfast and Colin made some coffee.

"Smells delicious." Colin nuzzled my neck from behind as I got out plates.

"Thank you. Old family recipe, you know." I winked and pointed to the packaging on the counter.

"I'm sure it's amazing. So when do we open presents?" He seemed particularly excited about that aspect. He almost seemed like a kid who was sure he was going to get that bike or gaming console. I kind of loved it.

"Well, we could wait until after rolls are done and we've had breakfast." Colin's face drooped, like the mere thought of having to wait was going to cause him physical pain.

"Or..." I began. And he lifted his head at that single word, like a lifeline to a drowning person.

"Yeah. Or?"

"Or we open presents tonight." The look on his face. Oh goodness. I couldn't help but laugh out loud. "I'm kidding! We can open gifts now if you'd like?" I was glad I hadn't taken a sip of coffee because I would've spit it right out. Colin's face brightened and he grabbed my hand and damn near dragged me into the living room.

Once I was sitting on the couch, he bounded to the tree like a rabbit.

"You're not excited, are ya?" I was laughing and practically snorting.

Gosh do I love this man!

"Well, ya, but it's cuz I can't wait 'til you open your gift," he came back to the couch handing me a small gift bag. I took it and waited.

"Oh, you want me to open it now? You don't want yours so we can open at the same time?"

"Ok, that works!" He made it to the tree and back in four steps. He sat down next to me on the edge, almost falling off the couch.

"Ok, on three we open together!" The excitement radiated from him.

"Deal."

"One, two, three!" He ripped the wrapping off like a crazed animal tearing into food. I opened the bag and pulled out the little black coin box. I was more interested in his reaction to the black and silver dog tags I got him than in what he got me.

Laughter was the last reaction I imagined getting, but that is exactly what Colin was doing: laughing. Not little gentle laughing, but like body shaking laughter.

"What? What's so funny?" I was getting nervous by the second.

"Open your box," he said, beaming.

I flipped open the coin box and I began laughing too. Inside was a set of black and silver dog tags.

"I guess great minds think alike?" I laughed and shook my head.

"Absolutely. I love you, Joleene," he said, kissing me with a smile on his face.

He put my tags on me while I put his on him and we both laughed more. We spent the rest of the morning enjoying the cinnamon rolls and coffee and every so often one or both of us would break out in laughter.

Later that evening we met up with Layla, Isaac, and Dale at the bar. I showed Layla my Christmas present and she just howled. She attempted to talk but couldn't catch her breath long enough. Colin showed Isaac who only howled louder.

"Definitely the best Christmas I have ever had," I said loud enough for everyone to hear.

"Here, here!" everyone responded as they raised their glasses.

Chapter 14

Before we knew it, the deployment window was upon us. I had no idea there was an actual time frame for a unit to head out. I just thought they all just left in one ginormous group.

"No, there is no way that could happen. We need to get in, go in stages. Otherwise we're a target, not to mention logistically speaking, moving that many soldiers, plus all the equipment and supplies...we need to go in stages." Colin explained one night after dinner.

"Yeah, that does make sense. That would be a nightmare to deal with."

Finally, the day came, Colin drove us to the company in his Jeep with all his gear stored in the back. The silence was almost deafen-ing. For the first time since our first date, nei-ther of us could find a way out of the awkward situation.

I have no idea what to say. How the hell do other wives do this once, let alone multiple times? This is torture. I hate this. I don't want to say goodbye.

My musing was interrupted by Bon Jovi. *Of course, the song would come on. Now timing sucks. And yet kind of poetic.*

Colin reached to turn it off, then thought bet-ter of it and only turned it down.

"I never realized how much I hated *goodbye* 'til now. It truly sucks," Colin stated matter of factly.

"Yeah, it really does," was my only response.

"It sounds so final. I mean, good-bye. It's like the verbal act of slamming the door on some-one. Good-bye. So final."

"Wow. Never saw it that way, but you're right. It does remind me of slamming shut a door. But what else could we say? I mean, we can't not say anything."

We drove in silence again. As we thought over the conversation, still silent, we passed through the main gate check and the silence stretched as we drove to the company.

Sighing, I stated, "Why don't you drive to the company and unload? Afterwards, I'll go park. That way you don't have to lug everything too far."

"You're sure? I don't mind."

"That's silly. Just pull up to company, unload, and then I'll go find a spot. That'll give you a chance to check in without wondering if you'll be on time." I looked at the dash clock. There was no chance he would be late. Even if we parked half a mile away. Check-in was in 90 minutes. Plenty of time.

"Okay. Yeah. That does make sense."

As I parked the Jeep and walked back to the company, our conversation played over in my head.

It's so final. It's like slamming a door shut. I hate it. Colin makes sense. But what do people say in this situation? Bye is just as bad? That sucks!

I continued my trek lost in my thoughts and playing with my set of dog tags Colin had gotten me. I was so lost in my thoughts, I was almost hit by a car from behind because I had drifted to the middle of the straightway in the parking lot. Their horn blaring startled me enough to jump out of the way.

"Are you all right, babe?" Evidently Colin had gotten all squared away and come to meet me, rushing over when he saw the near accident.

"Yeah, I guess I wasn't paying attention. Sorry."

"That's okay. He shouldn't have been such an asshole."

I stopped and stared at him. Colin had never really cussed in front of me before. "I think that's the first time you've ever cussed in front of me. Are you okay?"

"I'm fine. Sorry. I was taught not to curse in front of a lady, which is why I never do when you're around. But here"—he pointed back to the company—"that's a whole 'nother story. In fact, I'm apologizing now for what might pop out of my mouth. Please don't think less of me."

He had reached for my hand and pulled me to him.

"How could I? So what if you cuss a little, have you not heard me around Dale at the bar? Or how about on the phone with Layla? Seriously? They say cussing is a sign of high intelligence." I pulled from his embrace, winking and smiling. "Come on. We better get you back to company before Davis starts pitching a fit wondering where the hell you are."

"He wouldn't. But yeah, we should get back. Real quick first..." He pulled me to him again. "I won't be able to do this later. I love you Joleene. I hate that I never gave you a honeymoon, but I am so glad we got married when we did. I've never been so happy. I. Love. You." He punctuated each word with a kiss before passionately kissing me.

"I love you, Colin."

We headed back, holding hands, fingers locked together.

"You know, *see ya* isn't forever," I said out of the blue.

"What? Huh?"

"See ya. It gives the other person the feeling it won't be long before they see one another soon. It's not so final."

"Never thought of that, but yeah, you're right. It has a better ring to it. I like it," he said, kissing my hand. "But we don't have to say it just yet." His crooked smile was showing.

The next few hours were spent watching the guys ready their weapons and wondering every time we saw Davis, if formation would be called. At times, the tension in the air was palpable. Other times the guys were joking to help lighten the mood. Some of the wives were talking about their plans for the rest of the day as if this was just another training exercise. I was in awe at their lack of nerves.

"Honey, this is our fourth deployment. I figured out the best thing to do is to try to keep life as normal as possible. But I remember the first one; damn I was a wreck and probably looked like a hag. I was nothing but a ball of nerves. By the way, I'm Stacey. And this here is Keisha and Brittany—Britt for short. You're Dawson's bride, right?"

"Hi. Nice to meet you, I'm Joleene. Yeah, Colin—I mean Dawson—and I got married right before orders came down. So you've been through this three other times? I can't imagine going through this more than once!"

"Yep. Hey, come sit. It'll be awhile before formation is called." I sat down and got to know Stacy, Keisha, and Britt. I actually felt my shoulders relax listening to them. And all they talked about were their kids and what they were going to remodel in the house or what they might do for their next hair appointment. You know, normal conversation.

"So Joleene, we're thinking of planning a spa day in the next few weeks. Want to join us?" Keisha asked.

"Sure. And you can call me Jo. Almost everyone does except Colin." I smiled, but it was short-lived.

"Company, fall in!" Davis hollered.

Colin ran over and kissed me. "See ya, Joleene," he said with his eyes dancing above his famous, crooked smile before booking it to the formation.

"Wish Larry would do that."

"Yeah, Steve isn't that romantic. He even said, *bye babe* last night before bed, I wanted to slug him," Stacy stated. All I could do was smile, like a giddy schoolgirl.

"Company, attention!"

The sound of all the guys snapping to was like a clap of distant thunder, truly a sight to behold. Some big wig gave some instructions and then we heard it.

"Move out!"

And with that, a scramble of guys grabbing their gear and waving to their loved ones. Colin made sure to catch my eye and mouthed the words *I love you* then waved while giving his crooked grin. He turned and headed for the buses.

"All right, ladies, I've got to head out. Let's try to have dinner this week. Jo, give me your number and I'll call you later." Keisha pulled out her phone, as did Stacy and Britt. I gave them my number and we all went our separate ways. I lingered a bit and watched the buses leave.

"And so it begins, Jo, a new chapter." I sighed and headed for the jeep.

Chapter 15

*R*ing ring, ring ring!

I went running for the phone as I had done every time it rang for the last few weeks.

"H...hello?" I was panting from running.

"Joleene. You okay?" The sweetest sound of Colin on the other end. The tears fell as I smiled.

"Yes, I'm okay. I had to run to get the phone. Are you okay? Are you settled? Is everything fine? Oh, it's so good to hear your voice. I have missed you." I babbled on.

When I finally stopped, I could hear him chuckling. "Yes, babe. I'm fine. All settled. If that's what you call it. It's good to hear your voice too. I miss you. Are you okay? Not working all the time, are you?"

"I'm good." I giggled. "No. I'm not. Dale won't let me, but I have met up with Stacy and Keisha a few times and us three plus Britt are planning a spa day. I think next week. Layla has come over a few times too. I've stayed busy."

"Not too busy though."

"No, not too busy." I was again smiling as if he could see me.

"Good. Listen, babe. I only have a few minutes, but wanted to say hi and tell you I love you, Joleene. I miss you so much."

"I love you, Colin, and miss you tons. Please be safe."

"I will. See ya." I could hear him smile and almost see it in my mind.

"See ya, Colin."

It had been several weeks since I had seen Colin off. The first couple of weeks I wrote every day—just random thoughts and tidbits of what was going on, but I found myself not really repeating myself, just babbling. So my letters became more spaced out, every few days. During this time, I waited impatiently for something from Colin. I knew mail wasn't running yet, but that hadn't stopped me from damn near running to the mailbox every day in hopes that today would be the day I would hear from him, only to have those hopes dashed when nothing showed.

I found myself almost sulking as I headed back to my apartment with only bills or circulars in hand. Until one day, I saw a worn envelope mixed in with a few advertisements. I held the envelope in my left hand while my right glided over the handwritten address:

Mrs. Joleene Dawson

I closed my eyes and could see Colin's crooked smile and his steel-grey eyes winking at me saying, '*See I told ya I would write.*'

"Yeah, ya did. I'm just not that patient." I chuckled to myself as I headed back to the apartment reading the letter.

"Damn it." I slammed my phone down.

Layla looked up. "What?"

"I missed a call from Colin." The irritation was evident in my words.

"Oh," was all Layla said.

"Oh? Oh? That's all you have to say? Oh?" I about shouted the last word.

"What else do you want me to say? Honestly, I don't know what else to say, Jo."

"I know. I know. Sorry."

"When did you last hear from him?"

"Don't even know. Phones have been hit or miss."

"But you have letters, right?"

"I get a few at a time and then nothing for several days. And I'll get like three in one day. It's completely screwy. And it's driving me bonkers."

"Yeah. I'd prolly be a bit on edge too." She plopped down on the couch.

"This is crazy. We were told this would happen, but I guess I thought they were exaggerating."

Just then: *ring ring!*

"Hello? Colin?" I answered before the phone was fully up to my ear.

"Joleene."

That's all it took. I smiled and my shoulders relaxed. Layla excused herself to give me some privacy.

"Sorry. I missed your call. Somehow my phone got switched to silent. I'm so sorry. Is everything okay? Do you need me to send you anything? How are you? Damn I miss you."

Colin's laughter stopped my babbling. "I'm babbling again. Sorry."

"It's all good, babe. I rather like it when you babble." I could almost picture him laughing and shaking his head. "It's okay. I don't expect you to be able to answer every time I call. Everything is fine. Don't need anything special right now. I am fine. And I miss you. I do want to tell you something, but first I want you to take a breath." Sighing so he could hear me, I could hear him chuckling.

"Okay. Better?" he asked.

"Yes. So tell me what it is." I was audibly less tense.

"I just got word. I will be sent on RNR in July. So what do you want to do?"

"Yay! What do I want to do? Why are you asking me? You're the one stuck in some other country."

"Sandbox. We call it the sandbox. And I ask in case there was something on your mind. Honestly, I wouldn't mind checking into getting away for a few days. Maybe rent a cabin at The Land Between the Lakes. What do you think?"

"I think it sounds perfect. Do you have dates? I can make a reservation if you'd like."

"Not yet. And I'll take care of making reservations. I get some computer time." I could picture him winking. We'd had a few video chats over the last few months.

"It's settled. Once I get more info, I'll make arrangements and let you know so you can work something out with Dale. I hate to do this, babe, but we have a walk in a bit and I need to make sure I'm ready. I love you."

"Okay. I love you Colin. Be safe."

"Always. See ya, Joleene."

"See ya."

Click.

Chapter 16

"When are you heading up to LBTL?" Layla asked as we walked around Target.

"A few days after he gets in. He wanted to make sure if there was a delay in his flight, we wouldn't miss our reservation." Aimlessly, I put down an item and briefly looked up.

"Aren't you excited?"

"Yeah. Why?"

"Cuz, honestly you seem like you're dreading it. I mean, it's been like six months. I'd be dying to see my man. If I had one." She was giggling at her own statement.

"No, I'm...I'm excited, but nervous I guess. I mean it's been six months and we weren't married long before he left. What if he's changed his mind? I mean, seriously, we barely knew each other." I almost slammed another item down on the shelf, catching the attention of another customer.

"True. You weren't married long and yes, he could have changed his mind—"

"Gee, thanks. You're supposed to be my best friend and comfort me and tell me he'd be crazy to leave me, not agree with me!"

"Well, as I was saying, yes, he could have changed his mind, but I highly doubt it."

"How so?" I was a bit sheepish for cutting her off.

"Here's how." She pulled out her phone and searched for a picture. She flipped her phone so I could see her find. It was a picture of Colin watching me talking with someone at a Christmas party. He wasn't jealous, just an awe.

"Oh..." I had no words.

She flipped her phone back around and tapped a few buttons. Next thing I heard was my phone notifying me I had a message. "There, now you have it too. Sorry I didn't send it sooner. Honestly, I forgot. Isaac and I got to talking, but I'm glad I had it."

"Wait back up. You and Isaac were talking. When did this happen?"

"We started talking at the reception and just a few other times. He's called a couple of times since he left, but nothing serious. So nothing to talk about."

I sighed. "I'm being neurotic, aren't I?"

"Yep."

"But you let me."

"Yep."

"Why?"

"It's what you needed. Now are you finished so we can go shopping for your belated honeymoon?" She gave me a playful shove with her shoulder.

I nodded and grinned. "Yes."

"Good. But why are we at Target instead of Victoria's Secret? Come on, let's get out of here."

We left Target after we purchased a few items in the cart and spent the rest of the afternoon at the mall, shopping for my belated honeymoon.

****

The drive was perfect. We settled into our easy conversations while listening to various eighties songs on Sirius radio. The hour or so in the Jeep didn't seem all that long. I realized the picture Layla had taken all those months ago showed exactly how perfect we were for each other. At first, when we got to the campground, my facial expression betrayed my thoughts.

"Don't worry. We aren't camping in a tent or even a trailer. I booked a cabin." Colin chuckled as he parked the Jeep in front of the registration place and got out. "I'll be right back. Don't worry. I promise we booked a cabin."

I must have looked none too impressed, but seriously I was not the camping type. "We better have a cabin, or you'll be sleeping alone with the bears buddy," I mumbled to myself.

Colin got back in his Jeep after only a few minutes and handed me some paperwork. But the look on his face had me concerned.

"Don't tell me no cabin," I said, shaking my head. "I knew you were going to make me camp in a tent."

He looked at me intently, then the corners of his mouth turned upwards. "Ha fooled you!" he announced, holding up a key.

"Brat! That was *not* funny."

"Sure it was!" He was laughing as he dangled the key in front of me.

I snatched at the key and he pulled it away. I snatched at it again. Finally, I just turned in my seat, crossing my arms and huffing.

"Oh, come on. I had you going. And it was funny—at least from my point of view." He reached over to try and kiss me, but got my cheek instead.

He dangled the key again and let me grab it this time but held onto it.

I turned with a smile.

He kissed me and let go of the key.

Minutes later we were pulling up to the cabin. Absolute beauty didn't begin to describe the scene before me.

"Wow! This is gorgeous. Perfect getaway. Great idea, babe." I slowly got out of the

Jeep. Looking around, the nearest cabin was far enough away to be of no concern. Several people were playing various water activities on the lake from tubing to kayaking. People were walking about while others were hanging out by the shoreline. It was the middle of the afternoon on a Wednesday, so not as many people as a weekend, but it didn't matter. The area was so huge. There was enough room for everyone.

"I've lived within 90 minutes of this place and I've never been here. This is amazing! A little slice of heaven. How long are we here for?" The awe in my voice was very evident.

"Well, I booked for a few nights, but the guy told me we could stay 'til next Wednesday if we wanted. So we're here 'til then, if that's okay."

"Is that okay? Seriously, a whole week. We'll have to get more groceries, but I'm down. Can we unload later? Let's go walk around a bit."

Taking my hand, he answered my question. "I have missed our walks."

"Me too. I tried to go a few times to our park, but it wasn't the same. Too quiet, weird feeling, but this feels perfect." I wrapped around his arm and put my head on his bicep. As we walked, a deep breath of fresh air and his bodywash's scent helped relax the last residual tension I had built up over him coming home.

The week was great. We had our walks and campfires. We rented a paddleboat one afternoon and nearly flipped ourselves. We checked out the Homeplace 1850s Working Farm and Living Museum and saw a massive beaver nest in Beaver Marsh. We didn't jam pack our days, but we did spend every minute together.

One morning, I woke up just as the sun was rising. The water was like glass with mist rolling off. I saw a large eagle gliding in the air as if he was the only creature around. The soft pink of the eastern sky bled into the soft purple and deep blue of the western sky. The sun was just below the tree line creating a silhouetted scene.

I had been standing outside on the porch of the cabin and had left the door open, so I hadn't heard Colin get up and walk outside. It wasn't until he gently slid his arms around my waist that I registered him there.

"Isn't it gorgeous?"

"Yes, you are."

I tilted my head back slightly to catch him in the corner of my vision. "I meant the scenery."

"I know what you meant and you're right. It is beautiful. But the first sight I saw here was you, my love." He kissed me on the side of my forehead.

"I think we should come here every year. Don't you?" I nestled into his embrace.

"Absolutely. Maybe we can renew our vows here for our fifth anniversary." He squeezed me to him. I loved being in his arms. I could stay there forever.

"But for now, I say breakfast and cuddles."

"Deal. After you, Mrs. Dawson." His crooked smile let me know breakfast was not what he was thinking.

Damn do I love this man! Even looking like I rolled out of bed, a hot mess, he still finds me desirable and beautiful. I thought how lucky I was as I led him back inside and closed the door on the amazing creation outside.

****

The time of the cabin didn't fly by, but it wasn't long enough either. Soon after getting back to reality, Colin had to pack up and don his ACUs and army combat uniform once again.

It's crazy; as kids and even as adults, two weeks seems like more than enough time, but it really isn't, especially when it'll be months before you see the other person again.

We walked hand-in-hand, fingers entwined, to security check at Killeen Regional Airport. I tried to will him to slow down. Just before he went through security, he stopped and pulled me to him. He dropped his bag and my hand, placing each of his on either side of my face, and kissed me like there was no tomorrow and we only had this one moment to-gether. Time finally stood still. I held him with all my might.

When he finished, in a husky voice he whispered, "I love you, Joleene Nicole Dawson. See ya." That was it. The tears I had successfully held off fell of their own accord.

"I love you, Colin. See ya," I could barely whisper back. I just wanted to hold him forever, but he took a step back and grabbed his bag from the floor and turned. Just before he disappeared beyond security check he looked back with his crooked smile and steel-grey eyes and winked. Then he was gone.

July finished and melted into August. Colin called letting me know he made it safely to the *sandbox*. August came and went with no major hiccups. September rolled up unassumingly, hiding what was just beyond the horizon.

"You ok, girl?" Leyla shouted through the closed bathroom door at me.

"Yeah," I managed as I finished emptying my stomach for the third time that day. I rinsed out my mouth and nearly gagged in the process, but managed to keep from hacking up anymore.

I walked out of the bathroom and Layla was standing there. "What's wrong?"

"I don't know. My stomach has been giving me fits all day. I'm probably coming down with something like I always do this time of year."

"Maybe." Layla just stood there looking at me, raising an eyebrow. "You sure?"

"Yeah. It's nothing." I walked back to the living room and sat slowly down as if I was trying not to hurt myself.

Unfortunately, my butt never hit the cushions before I stood up and ran back into the bathroom.

"I'm gonna run and get you some crackers and a Sprite. You don't have any."

I just leaned against the wall opposite the toilet, willing my stomach to stop rolling. I was hoping I was done so I could at least lie down. Eventually, I made it back to the couch and just laid my head back, taking deep breaths in hopes of settling myself and staving off a headache.

I hate getting sick. I was trying to focus on my breathing instead of the acrobatics my stomach was attempting. *I'm probably going to have to call off tomorrow. I'll have Layla call Dale when she gets back. Damn. I hope she hurries.* I could feel another round coming.

I heard Layla call out as I closed the bathroom door. When I came back out, she had a spread of various items on the coffee table, including crackers and a Sprite already opened and poured over ice with a straw—she knew me well. And there was one other item that confused me.

"Call it a hunch. Get something to drink first." She knew what had caught my attention without me saying a word. I looked at her, then back at the box, then back at her, then back to the box, shaking my head.

"No way, not possible. I had my period—"I stopped walking to the couch and raised my hands slowly to my mouth. I remembered I hadn't had my period since before Colin was home. I had just brushed it off as stress related. I mean seriously, what did *I* have to stress about?

She simply grabbed the box and handed it over. I booked it back to the bathroom. Three minutes later, I walked slowly out holding the test. I just looked at Layla. She met me halfway and guided me to the couch. I was clearly in shock.

"How..." I started then swallowed hard. "How, how did this happen?" I was staring blankly at the room.

"Well, at some point when Colin was home, you two started kissing and holding each other. That led to—" She stopped when I smacked her in the arm.

"I know *how*, smart ass." I was looking at her as she grinned back.

"What? You asked! I thought I'd remind you of health class." She shrugged.

I grabbed my Sprite and crackers and sat back on the couch.

"What am I going to do?"

"Well, I would say first you eat that cracker and take a sip of your Sprite. Then I'd suggest calling Dale to let him know you need tomorrow off and then call your doctor for an appointment."

"Funny you say that." I took a sip of my Sprite and waited a moment to see if my sprinting abilities would be needed.

"I was going to have you call him for me, figuring I would need to rest."

"Deal. I'll call him right now," she said, reaching for her phone and dialing before I could tell her she didn't have to.

"Don't tell him!"

"I won't. Go call your doctor and make that appointment."

Layla made sure I was okay before leaving me to rest, promising me she'd be by in the morning to pick me up from my appointment. I spent the night in disbelief. Sleep found me before I could make it to the bedroom.

Chapter 17

It had been a week since I discovered I was going to be a mom. I called off work and told Dale I wasn't feeling well, which was partly true. He grumbled, but told me to take care. I knew if I showed up to work, he would know something was up and get me to tell him. But I wanted to tell Colin first.

When my phone rang, I jumped. I had been staring at the ultrasound, clearly showing I was pregnant. I tried to slow my breathing as I answered my phone.

"Hello?" I must have sounded slightly winded still because on the other end I heard Colin start laughing. "Running for the phone again, babe?"

"No, it just startled me is all."

"What's up, Joleene?" He stopped laughing immediately.

"I need to tell you something and I'm not sure how to or how you're going to react."

"Okay …"

I could tell he was tensing up. His reaction only added to my nerves. Taking an audibly deep breath, I forged ahead. We had never discussed having a family. So I was unsure how he would take the news he was going to be a father. I took one look at the ultrasound and simply stated,

"I'm pregnant."

Silence was all that greeted me. I thought we had gotten disconnected. So I looked at my phone. Nope. It was still connected.

"Colin, are you there? Did you hear me? Please say something." The silence stretched on. I looked at my phone again. "Colin. Please say something." The tears were welling up and threatening to fall. "Colin." My voice cracked.

"Are you sure?" was all he said. Silent tears slid down my cheek.

"Yes. I saw the doctor last week and I'm holding a picture from the ultrasound."

"Really?" His voice sounded different, disbelief but not disappointment or irritation. "Really? We're going to have a baby?" Excitement came over the line.

I lifted my head. *He's happy. He's not upset. Or accusing me of stepping out on him.*

"Joleene you there? You okay?" His concerned tone penetrated my thoughts.

"Yes. I'm here. I'm fine. I just"—I stopped mid-thought—"I just thought—"

"You thought what?"

"I just thought when you didn't answer, you were upset." I was crying ugly tears by this point.

"How could I be upset? You're having our child. I'm sorry I didn't respond at first. I thought it was a dream. Then I thought you were joking. Oh, Joleene, I'm sorry I upset you. I, I wish I was there. I'd pick you up and spin you around kissing you."

"If you did that, we'd both need to change. As I puke all over us." I instinctively put my hand on my stomach as the very thought turned it and threatened to end our conversation.

"I wouldn't care. Oh, Joleene. I'm so happy. I may not sleep tonight."

"Just make sure you stay focused on your next mission."

"No worries there. I love you."

"I love you."

"I'm sorry, babe, but I have to go, but I'm so excited to talk more about us and the baby. I wish I could be there, but I'll be involved as much as I can. I love you, Joleene."

"I wish you were here too, be safe. I love you, Colin."

Click.

Chapter 18

Every new year brings new beginnings and this year for me was no different. I was nearing the end of my second trimester of what could only be considered a textbook healthy pregnancy.

Colin's unit was preparing for redeployment. Their time in the *sandbox* was finally coming to an end. I was so excited. I was moving into a two-bedroom apartment in the same complex that weekend. Dale and Layla and movers were coming over to help.

Over the last several months, Dale had become like a proud uncle-to-be and even more overprotective. On busy nights, he kept me behind the bar and had a stool put back there so I could sit down. It was quite comical at times to listen or watch him when I was around.

Layla had been beyond amazing. She listened to me bawl for no reason. She went baby shopping and had made sure to inform me that she would be Auntie Layla. She had every intention of spoiling this child.

The day before the move had started like any other. I was putzing around before I finished the lightweight packing Dale and Layla had allowed me to do, listening to the classic 80s station on my new Alexa I had gotten for Christmas. Smiles and horrible singing with some eighties dance moves. I was on top of the   world.

I wasn't ready for a knock at the door.

Knock, knock, knock,

"Coming. Alexa, volume down." The music lowered.

"Hell—" my smile dropped instantly as I opened the door and saw two soldiers on the other side, my hand went to my mouth and the other dropped from the handle.

"No, no." I started shaking my head.

"Ma'am, may we come in?"

I just stood there, unable to move.

"Ma'am?"

I backed away from the door. I reached out behind me for something to grab. I felt faint. The soldiers must have sensed and tried to help me to the couch, but I just kept backing away. I finally found a chair and stumbled into it. "Ma'am." They came over, but not too close.

"Jo," was all I could utter.

"The commandant of the United States Army has entrusted me to express his deep regret that your husband, Colin, was killed in action in Mosul, Iraq on 15 January, when his squad was ambushed. The commandant extends his deepest sympathy to you and your family in your loss."

I sat numb.

"Ma'am," he repeated.

"Jo, please call me Jo." My voice sounded hollow to my ears as I sat there staring.

"Ma'am is there someone you can call or we can find to help you? Parents? Family?"

"I have no family. My best friend is coming over. I'm moving tomorrow." Unconsciously, my hand drifted to my swollen belly.

"Ma'am do we need to call a doctor? Are you okay?" Layla had come through the door, chatting on the phone. The sight of the soldiers stopped her in her tracks. Seeing me in the chair in a catatonic state, Layla must have known in an instant what happened.

Colin had been killed.

Layla immediately called Dale, who was over within minutes. They both talked to the officers, keeping a close eye on me. I hadn't said a word. I just sat in the chair, staring into space.

Over the next few weeks, Layla stayed with me, only leaving when Dale could be there, neither trusting to leave me alone. They helped me move as planned. They took me to the funeral, though I didn't say much.

I moved about as if someone had hijacked my body. A few times, I showed some life, but it was short-lived. Once in the middle of the night, about six weeks after the news, Layla found me in the master closet, unpacking

Colin's clothes. Dale and Layla had chosen not to do anything with Colin's clothes until I was better. But I couldn't handle it.

"What are you doing, girl?" She was yawning and trying to wipe the sleep from her eyes.

"What's it look like? I'm hanging up Colin's clothes. He'll be home soon. Why are you still here? You should've gone home before you fell asleep, silly."

Layla stared at me for a few moments, her face contorting as she debated her response. "Come on, sweetie. I'll help you in the morning. Right now it's the middle of the night. You need sleep." Coaxing me back to bed, Layla stayed until I was asleep.

Chapter 19

February bled into March and then April, all passing in a blur. I was barely aware of time. April 15th, Tax Day. It began like any other day for the last several months. I shuffled around the apartment, walked past my Alexa, and stopped for a moment. I opened my mouth to request something. Then I closed it again and kept walking. I walked to the baby's room. Dale had set up the crib the other day, but that was it. No theme or design had been decided upon. I didn't even know if I was having a boy or a girl. I was supposed to find out when Colin got home, but I had canceled the appointment.

I shuffled to my room and sat on the bed. It looked like a tornado had whipped through the blankets. I used to make my bed daily, but it had been months. Honestly, it had been months since I had done anything.

Dale and Layla had done what they could to keep food in the apartment and simple house tasks done but there were still boxes everywhere waiting to be unpacked. I used to be on top of all this, not OCD, but orderly. Now I didn't notice the chaos around me. The days I worked, I got myself showered and dressed and went through my shift on autopilot. When I didn't work, I shuffled aimlessly from room to room throughout the day.

Today was no different until a sharp pain made me blink a few times as if trying to focus.

I drew in a sharp breath and held it until the pain subsided. I sat for a few minutes more before getting up and shuffling back to the kitchen. Another wave of pain shot through my body, forcing me to stop and lean against the wall. Once the pain let up, I headed to the kitchen to get some water and then to sit down. Before I got to the couch, another stabbing sensation ripped through me, causing me to call out when I could finally make a sound.

I called Layla. "I think something is wrong," I said as soon as Layla picked up.

"I'll be right there."

Click.

A few more throbs came and went before Layla let herself in.

"Tell me what's going on," she said as she walked in.

I told her, and as I was telling her, she began walking around the apartment like she was looking for something.

"What are you doing?" I was confused as I watched her flit around the apartment, like a bee going from flower to flower.

"I'm looking for your go bag."

"My what?"

"Your hospital bag. I'm pretty sure you're in labor."

"I don't have one." Layla stopped in her tracks.

"What do you mean you don't have one?"

"I don't have anything packed."

"Why?" Her voice was quickly turning into that matronly voice adults get when a kid does something not necessarily wrong, but not smart.

"I don't know. Figured I'd throw some stuff together when I needed to." I shrugged my shoulders and sucked in a deep breath as another sharp pain came.

"Oh. Kay. What do you want to pack? Just tell me and I'll get it." I told her the usual items: toiletries, extra clothes, a pillow.

"Where's the baby's coming home outfit, blanket, car seat, diaper bag?"

"I don't have it." I looked at her ready to burst into tears.

"What, you don't have an outfit? Oh, no worries." She waved me off.

"No, I don't have any of it". By this point, the tears began to stream down.

Oh my gosh. I'm an awful mom. Before the baby's born. I have nothing. The crib is set up. That's it? The tears fell harder.

Layla could see my thoughts across my face and ran to me and took my hands.

"No, you are not horrible. Listen to me." She pulled my hands to force my body to face her and looked me in the eyes. "You are not bad. You've had a very rough few months. You've been in pure survival mode and that is okay. Don't worry about that. We'll help you. You'll figure it out. Hey, it's okay." She hugged me, shushing me and my tears as I silently balled. Another stabbing pain broke the moment.

"Okay. We have the basics and that's fine. Once you can stand, we'll head out." She squeezed my hand.

By the time I got settled in my labor and delivery room, Dale had showed up, but it wasn't until I saw Isaac that I really cried. I mean, ugly cried. It had been the first time I had seen him since he got back. I had missed a welcome home ceremony.

"How am I supposed to do this?" I asked through ugly sobs and contractions.

"Like every other woman on the planet has done since the dawn of time." Layla wiped my face.

"No. How am I going to raise this child? I can't do this on my own. This baby is never going to know who their father is or was. I can't do this."

In stereo, Dale and Isaac answered. "Yes, they will know who Colin was. We all will make sure of it."

"You can do this, Joleene, and you are not alone. We are all here." Layla had never called me Joleene. Not in all the years we'd known each other.

"You've never called me that."

"What, Jo? I've always called you Jo."

"No, you said Joleene. In fact, no one ever called me Joleene except Colin."

But before any of us could think about her slip of the tongue, another contraction hit, causing me to yell out as my doctor came in.

"Well, now, looks like we have a full house. Who do we have here?"

"Hello sir." Isaac piped up before I could even form a thought. "The father was my best friend and I wanted to be here for Jo. She's family. And this here," he continued, pointing to Dale, "is her brother."

"Oh, that's nice of you two to stop by." Then, turning his focus on me, he asked, "How are you feeling, Jo?"

Trying to take a deep breath was no easy feat. "I'm okay. I guess." I was struggling to adjust to a more comfortable position.

"Well, let's check how you're doing." As the doctor went to check on my progress, Isaac and Dale averted their eyes.

"We'll be right outside if you need us, Jo." They both about tripped over each other trying to get out of the room while looking at the ceiling. It was quite comical to watch.

After checking me, the doctor said, "Wow. You're about seven centimeters. I'd say within the next few hours, you will meet your little one. Let's get a hold of anesthesiology for an epidural stat and make sure we are fully prepped," he called to the nurses. "Don't worry, Jo. We'll see if we can't help you be a little bit more comfortable."

"Okay"—my response was cut off by another contraction.

A little while later the anesthesiologist showed up, but before he could administer my epidural, my water broke and the nurses began checking to make sure everything was fine.

"Get the doctor! This baby is coming. Now!" Evidently I had progressed faster than anyone anticipated, myself included.

Ten minutes later, Layla was cutting the cord and the nurse was placing my newborn on my chest. Tears flowed like a waterfall.

As I held this precious baby in my arms, all I could think of was how amazing this child already was. Just as the nurse was asking for his name, he opened his eyes. My breath caught; staring back at me was Colin.

"What?"

"What is his name?"

"*His* name? I have a son?" I stared at this precious little baby who had his father's eyes just moments after being born. "CJ, Colin Anthony Dawson Jr., after his father."

I spent the next few days recovering from the fast and furious arrival of CJ. It felt surreal. I held him most of the time and every time he opened his eyes, my breath would catch. No one would ever doubt who his daddy was. He looked just like Colin.

When I wasn't holding CJ, I was staring at him. Layla stayed the first night to make sure I was all right. Dale and Isaac stopped by with balloons and a giant teddy bear wearing a beret. Isaac made sure the insignia was correct. Britt, Stacey, and Keisha stopped by too. Evidently Isaac made sure to get the word out to the company about CJ's birth.

There weren't many visitors per se, but between them and nurses and doctors, I hadn't been alone more than a few minutes at a time. I hadn't a chance to even begin to process, let alone accept, that I was a parent. A single parent.

"Well, little guy, it's just you and me, I guess." It was during one of the brief times I was alone and holding him. "I have no idea what I'm doing. I'll be honest. And I'm not sure what's going to happen tomorrow when they discharge me because I don't have a car seat for you yet." The tears began to well up. "I'm so sorry, CJ. I'm already messing up. I should have had everything ready for you. But I don't."

My head dropped forward as the tears flowed freely. I don't know for how long I sat like that, silently crying before I heard Layla's voice.

"Oh, girl. What's wrong? CJ okay? Do I need to get the nurse?" Panic was rising in her voice.

"No, he's fine. He's asleep. I'm just apologizing for already messing up and telling him I wasn't sure what would happen tomorrow."

"Tomorrow?"

"Yeah, when they discharge me. They told me I would be leaving tomorrow, but because I don't have a car seat, CJ won't be allowed to leave." Fresh tears flowed as I finally looked up from staring at him and saw Layla holding this car seat fully decked out, complete with a few toys hanging on the handle, a shark and an octopus, with a green camo canopy.

"Where did you get that?" I choked out the words between sobs.

"I didn't. Isaac brought it over. The company chipped in and bought this and a stroller."

"What, why?" I blinked trying to clear my vision.

"They said it was because Colin provided cover fire that so many were able to seek cover. He saved their lives, Jo, and they wanted to thank you." Layla's voice cracked as she sat down on the couch.

"I had no idea. I never heard what happened."

"Sweetie. They told you. I was there. And it was mentioned at the funeral too. You just never heard what they said." She took a steadying breath. "But hell, I don't think I would have either. You did what you had to to survive and that's okay. But now you have CJ. You can't lock yourself up, so to speak." Getting up and coming over to the bed, she laid a hand gently on his lumbering head.

"He needs you."

Chapter 20

The next day was a bit hectic. Paperwork, newborn pictures, fitting CJ in his new car seat and packing everything up. But finally, we were all buckled up in Layla's car and heading home.

"Hey, can you stay a bit to help me at least move the crib and some boxes?" I asked Layla. "I know you prolly want to get home and rest. So, I get it if you want to head out."

"I can stay for a bit and you don't need to get it all set up today. Remember, you've just had a baby three days ago. You're still recovering. We'll move a few boxes out of the way out of any walk path and leave the crib where it's at. Okay?"

I started to shake my head and tell her *no*, but she silenced me.

"Yes. Trust me. You need to rest too. Don't argue with me." She stared at me through the rearview mirror as I sat next to CJ in the backseat.

Once we got to my complex, I realized Layla had been right. I was sore as I tried to maneuver CJ out of the car without waking him and I was suddenly tired.

"Okay. We'll just move the boxes from CJ's room. All of a sudden I'm wiped." I stifled a yawn.

"No worries. You get in and I'll move the boxes out of the way. Then you go rest." Layla opened the door and let me go first.

The first thing I noticed was the fresh clean smell. Then I realized my apartment had been fully cleaned and the boxes in the main areas had been unpacked and the contents taken care of. Pictures had been hung. It looked like a home and not an apartment someone was staying in. I slowly walked around while holding CJ. I was speechless.

"Wha...who? When?" My words stuck as I saw my wedding picture. I glanced away and headed towards the bedrooms. No more boxes lined the walls. There was even a vase on the dining table with flowers. Everywhere I turned, something caught my eye.

"We decided a clean slate was in order. Isaac and a few guys came in and cleaned everything top to bottom. I'll tell you, these guys should start a company because *damn!* Me and a few ladies set to work, taking care of the main areas." She followed me to the bedrooms. First, I went to my room. My bed was made and the floor was cleared. There were a few boxes in the corner, but I knew why they were still there. Layla didn't even mention them.

"Wow!" was all I could say. My bed looked so inviting. "Let's get CJ to bed. It's been too much for me. I think a nap is needed." I yawned.

"Sure. I'll go move the boxes."

As she headed off to CJ's room at the end of the hall, I looked once more around the room, spying the boxes. *A task for another day*. And I left the room.

"Layla, I'm coming," I called as loud as I dared with CJ still asleep in my arms. I stopped short just inside his room. Instead of finding a white crib set up in the middle of the room with a few boxes scattered around, I walked into a fully set up and decorated nursery. A rocking chair sat by the window with a little table next to it. There was a book-shelf opposite the window with some knick-knacks and books set up. The bear from Dale and Isaac was sitting in a little nook with a few other stuffed animals. The crib had been moved to the wall parallel to the window with a new matching changing table and dresser next to it. There were pictures up and the let-ters CJ in green camo on the wall where the door was. A little table and chair set was set on the other wall. It was better than I could have ever hoped for.

"Layla..."

She came over, gently took CJ and placed him in his crib.

"I told you we wanted a fresh start for you where you could focus on CJ and you."

"But this had to take forever. And I was only gone three days. How did you manage this?"

"Well, it didn't take forever, but it did take an army. Isaac got the guys together, like I said, and I got some of the ladies together and we managed to give you the baby shower you didn't want." She winked at me. "We love you, Jo. And we are here for you."

She squeezed me. "Now let's get you to bed. So you have a chance to rest before CJ wakes." She led me back to my room.

Chapter 21

The next several weeks were spent in a blur for me and CJ as I tried to figure out the whole mother-son thing. Sleep was as precious as gold. Between feedings and diaper changes and the endless loads of laundry and walks to settle CJ, I tried to rest when I could, but also tried to maintain the apartment.

I had moved the boxes in the corner of my room to my closet, which looked like someone had torn through in a moment of pure panic or mania. Boxes half-filled, clothes strewn here and there. All in all, it was a helter skelter mess.

"Tomorrow," I would say and turn out the light. But tomorrow brought a look of unease and *tomorrow* was whispered again and again.

****

One Saturday in June, Layla stopped by and announced she was kidnapping her nephew for the day. I just looked at her.

"Seriously. I'm taking CJ out for an auntie and CJ day. Let's get him packed. And before you say anything, no, you can't come." She stuck her tongue out at me when I put my hands on my hips.

Dropping my hands, I said, "Fine, I was just going to go check on him and see if he was up from his morning nap." I walked off.

"Perfect!" The excitement eked out of her voice.

She got CJ changed while I packed his diaper bag. He giggled at something Layla did. She loved him and he adored his auntie. If truth be told, I was grateful.

"So what am I supposed to do while y'all are partying and painting the town?"

"Whatever you want. Take a bubble bath, relax, veg out. Whatever. Turn on your eighties music and rock out."

My 80s music. It had been months since I listened to anything. Not since that day. In fact, I hadn't played anything on my Alexa since. It sat there in my room waiting to answer my request.

"His bag ready?" Layla called out, disturbing my thoughts.

"Yep. Here you go. You sure about this? I can be ready in 10." I kissed CJ's head.

"I'm sure. No mama allowed."

With that, they headed out the door for the afternoon adventure leaving me alone.

"Alexa, play soft ballads from the 80s," I stated as I sat on the floor in the middle of my master closet. I was surrounded by the daunting task of spring cleaning. I hated spring cleaning. It never seemed to end. I always have way more crap to get rid of than I expect. Talk about anxiety, I have to psyche myself up for like a week before I even get started. You would think by now, I wouldn't have an issue, but I do.

Alexa began playing Guns 'n Roses as I continued to sit and stare blankly at the junk piled up. Pulling my knees up and resting my head on them I just listened as Axl Rose belted out the words to "Sweet Child O' Mine". Taking a deep breath, I hear the words, "Sweet child,

Sweet child of mine," finishing the song.

"Well, this crap won't clear itself out. Might as well as get to it."

I stood up and started with the top shelf. I pulled down an old shoe box full to the brim of pictures and trinkets. The lid was just sitting on top, not even properly on because it was so full. Just as I was lifting the top, Bon Jovi comes on with "Sitting here wasted and wounded at this old piano..." and I see a picture of me laughing and instantly I am transported back to The Screaming Eagle bar. The memories from the moment I first saw him to the last played like a movie reel through my mind. It was time to accept that he was really gone. The tears I hadn't really allowed myself to cry finally came out like a typhoon. Not like the numbness from before. Not even like the tough exterior I had been putting up for CJ. Now, alone, I just let myself truly grieve. The tears guided me through both grief and healing as the song played.

As Jon Bon Jovi's voice faded, I wiped my eyes and breathed. Colin would have wanted me to move on. To find happiness again. Not just for CJ. But for myself.

As Def Leppard broke through with "Pour Some Sugar on Me", I placed the pictures back in the box, stood and placed the box on the upper shelf. I began going through the clothes strewn everywhere and half hung up. I packed up Colin's clothes and neatly closed the box. I labeled it. I wasn't ready to get rid of it yet, but it was time to put it up. Slowly I got to where I could see my floor. Then I could actually hang up clothes without teetering over a pile of stuff. Finally, I came to the three boxes.

These had been left alone by everyone who helped set up the apartment when CJ was born. These were the boxes of Colin's personal effects from the *sandbox*. I took a deep breath and closed my eyes.

Oh, Colin. I wish you were here. CJ is growing up so fast. I see more and more of you in him. The other day I swear he gave me the same crooked smile that always made me smile. How do I do this without you? Layla, Dale, and Isaac are great, but they aren't you. I'd give anything to feel your arms around me again, or your fingers intertwined with mine or here you call me Joleene.

I took another breath, opened my eyes and opened the first box. Some of his uniforms—oh, they stunk. His extra boots, worse than the uniforms, and a few other items. I packed them all back up and resealed the box as fast as possible. I'd see if Isaac knew what I could do with them.

The second box was just miscellaneous items. Like some of his personal gear, a flashlight, earbuds, a couple of pocket knives with his duffle wadded up at the bottom. I tossed the ear buds and set aside the bag for a CJ for when he was older. The rest I put on top of the stinky box for Isaac.

The last box took me by surprise upon opening. There was a sealed envelope... the one Dale had handed Colin at our wedding reception. I gasped as I opened it to find a few hundred dollar bills. '*Oh, Dale...*' How could I ever thank or repay him? I knew what he'd say... it was a gift. It was exactly what I needed to get back on my feet.

Then, I saw his journal. I slowly picked it up as if it was a fragile vase. Holding it in one hand, my other spread over the front cover. I had forgotten about it. I walked back into the bedroom, intent on putting it in my nightstand when something fell out. I picked it up. It was one of the letters I had sent him. I opened the journal to replace the letter and was greeted by other letters and a few pictures of us and a picture of me showing off my baby bump. I smiled. I turned to the first page and read,

> Oh, it is great to be writing again. Joleene bought me this beautiful journal and I love it. I smiled thinking about how she knew it

was silly. She'll never know how grateful I am. She found this for me...

I turned a few pages and found more writings and I flipped to somewhere near the middle. The date made my breath catch. September 10th. The day I told him I was pregnant. I dropped to the bed as I began to read.

I find myself in awe. Joleene just told me she's pregnant. She thought I would be mad. I feel the total opposite, but I upset her when I didn't respond right away. But how was I supposed to respond? We never discussed starting a family, but WOW! I'm going to be a father. Joleene is going to be an amazing mother. She really is. How amazing is it going to be! I'll miss a few things, but I'll be there for the birth.

I am going to be a dad!

Tears welled up as I read those last words, which he had written in all caps. He was excited. How could I have ever thought he wouldn't be? I flipped the page to where the bookmark was, it had been his last entry. Because mail had stopped, it was a letter to me:

Joleene,

Only a few more weeks and I'll be back stateside and in your arms. I can hardly wait. I can't wait to see your beautiful smile and to make you blush. Though I have loved the pictures, it's just not the same. I can't hold a picture like I can hold you. I hope you don't mind, but when I next hold you, I am not letting go.

I am excited to see if we're having a boy or a girl. If we're having a girl, I know she'll be just as beautiful as her mama. If it's a boy, I can only hope he's as ruggedly handsome as I am not.

I know you're worried about being a mother, but I know you're going to be amazing. Our child and hopefully their siblings are going to be so blessed to have such a great mom. You've asked how you're supposed to be a good mom a few times. Babe, you already are. Look at you. You have been independent for years, taking care of all those around you. You married me and stuck with me when most women bail during separations like this. When you found out you were pregnant, you made sure I was okay with it. You've dealt with this pregnancy almost entirely on your own. I don't know another who could have had your experiences and still be as beautiful and kind-hearted as you are Joleene.

You are a wonderful mom already. You just need to see it and believe it yourself.

Sorry, I kind of rambled a bit. Note to self, don't try to write a heartfelt letter when you've been up for over 24 hours. Anyways. I love you Joleene and miss you. Can't wait to hold you again.

See ya,

Colin.

I don't even remember voicing any concerns about being a mom. It's like you heard my thoughts the last several months, Colin. I, taking a few steadying breaths, *I have felt so inadequate to be both mother and father to CJ. I have missed you so much, but I know you wouldn't want me to isolate myself and keep myself locked in my own mind. You would want me to live, to have adventures, to show CJ the world. You would want me to love again. You will always be here, Colin, but I have to stop looking to the past and focus on the here and now to look forward with excitement to the future. I will always love you Colin and I will do everything I can to teach CJ all about who you were, but he and I need to live too. I love you, Colin. Goodbye.*

I closed the journal and placed it in the open drawer of my nightstand. I finished combing through the third box, packed it up and put it next to the shoe box on the shelf.

Cindi Lauper's "Time After Time" was just finishing and Huey Lewis came on with the "Power of Love". I smiled. And for the first time in what seemed like forever, I believed everything was going to be alright. *I* was going to be alright.

The End

THANK YOU

I cannot thank you enough for reading Serendipity! I hope you enjoyed it as much as I enjoyed writing it.
Would you consider leaving your honest review on the book page? I would greatly appreciate your input!

Please go to:

Thank you again for choosing Serendipity, I look forward to seeing you around in the future books.